Then she heard the creak of wicker as he leaned back in the rocker and a male sigh of contentment that made her toes curl in her tennis shoes.

Daring to turn her head, she watched him rocking slowly, his mouth curled into a small smile as he looked out over the bay.

The shiver of desire made her turn her gaze back to the water in a hurry. "It's so peaceful out here."

"Most of the time," he said softly. "My family can be loud at times, but I guess you'll find that out yourself. I mean, don't get me wrong. It's all love. But it gets loud, and my mom and Gram can push each other's buttons like nobody's business."

"It sounds like you're trying to warn me, but I have to confess that a loving but loud family doing a renovation together makes for great television." She leaned her head back and rocked her chair in time with his. "The fun really starts tomorrow."

"I can't wait," he replied without an ounce of sincerity in his voice.

Chuckling softly, she watched the rain fall and tried to convince that panicky voice inside her head that, no, she had *not* gotten herself in over her head here.

She was almost sure of it.

Dear Reader,

Welcome back to Blackberry Bay, New Hampshire!

If there's one thing we have a lot of in New England, it's old, historical houses with a lot of character, and in *The Home They Built*, I got to write about two women who love old houses as much as I do. Tess Weaver is struggling to maintain her home, and brings Anna Beckett and her show, *Relic Rehab*, to town to help her remodel it. Anna has made saving historical properties into her livelihood, but she's never met a woman like Tess. And she's never met a man like Tess's grandson, Finn Weaver. He makes it hard to concentrate not only on her job, but on the real reason she's in town.

You can find out what I'm up to and keep up with book news on my website, www.shannonstacey.com, where you'll find the latest information, as well as a link to sign up for my newsletter. And you can also reach me by emailing shannon@shannonstacey.com or look me up on Facebook at Facebook.com/shannonstacey.authorpage.

I hope you enjoy Anna and Finn's story, and your visit to Blackberry Bay.

Happy reading!

Shannon

www.ShannonStacey.com

The Home They Built

SHANNON STACEY

HARLEQUIN

SPECIAL
EDITION

Recycling programs
for this product may
not exist in your area.

ISBN-13: 978-1-335-40466-4

The Home They Built

Copyright © 2021 by Shannon Stacey

This edition published by arrangement with Harlequin Books S.A.

For questions and comments about the quality of this book,
please contact us at CustomerService@Harlequin.com.

Harlequin Enterprises ULC
22 Adelaide St. West, 40th Floor
Toronto, Ontario M5H 4E3, Canada
www.Harlequin.com

Printed in U.S.A.

A *New York Times* and *USA TODAY* bestselling author of over forty romances, **Shannon Stacey** grew up military and lived many places before landing in a small New Hampshire town where she has resided with her husband and two sons for over twenty years. Her favorite activities are reading and writing with her dogs at her side. She also loves coffee, Boston sports and watching too much TV. You can learn more about her books at www.shannonstacey.com.

Books by Shannon Stacey

Harlequin Special Edition

Blackberry Bay

More than Neighbors
Their Christmas Baby Contract

Carina Press

Boston Fire

Heat Exchange
Controlled Burn
Fully Ignited
Hot Response
Under Control
Flare Up

The Kowalski Series

Exclusively Yours
Undeniably Yours
Yours to Keep
All He Ever Needed
All He Ever Desired

Visit the Author Profile page
at Harlequin.com for more titles.

For my husband, for being my port in the storm that was a very challenging year. I'm always thankful I get to go through this life with you.

Chapter One

"You are not even going to believe what your grandmother did now."

Finn Weaver wasn't sure how many conversations with his parents had begun with those words, but he'd put his money on at least half of them. "It can't be that bad, Mom. On a scale of going to the market in her pajamas to the time she got a pet goat and tried to train it to live in the house, how bad is it?"

His mother sighed, and it sounded loud even over the phone. "If she bought an entire herd of goats and knit them matching sweater vests—no, if she *stole* the goats matching sweater vests from the ski shop—it still wouldn't be as bad as what she's done now."

"Hold on. Let me sit down." Finn walked across his office and sat in his plush leather executive chair, spinning it to look out over the view of the Piscataqua River.

"I don't think sitting down is going to help," she said.

"Does she need bail money?"

"I wish it were that simple."

That didn't sound good. "What's worse than Gram being arrested?"

"Well, let's start with the fact she expects you to come home for a few weeks to aid and abet her."

"You mean that figuratively, right?" When it came to Gram, he could never be sure.

"Literally," his mother snapped. "We all get to take part in defrauding a popular television show in a way that's definitely wrong and probably criminal."

That didn't make any sense. While Gram's shenanigans could be legendary, neither of his parents had ever even had a speeding ticket. They didn't *do* shenanigans. "We're not taking part in that. I'll call her and talk her out of whatever it is she's up to."

"She already signed the contract."

Groaning, Finn leaned forward so he could rest his forehead on his hand. He should probably take some preemptory ibuprofen because this was going to be one hell of a headache. "I feel like *defrauding* and *criminal* are the words I should be focusing on, but, to be honest, I'm a little hung up on the expectation I can just drop everything and hang out in Blackberry Bay for a few weeks."

"It gets better." His mom paused, as if waiting for his reaction, but he couldn't manage more than a weary sigh. "She needs you here by ten tomorrow morning."

Gram had a bad habit of waiting until the last second to drop bombs because it didn't give a person time to get out of the way. And no matter how often her loved ones complained, she didn't change her strategy, because it was effective.

He looked up, his gaze fixed not on the river this time, but on his own faint reflection in the window. He *looked* like a grown man. Dark hair kept neatly trimmed. His suit coat hung by the door and his shirt sleeves were rolled up, but he was still wearing the boring maroon tie. It was the reflection of a professional adult who had a business to run.

But it didn't show the grandson on the inside who had a soft spot for the woman who kept their lives in a constant state of low-level disarray, with occasional spikes of straight-up chaos. There was nothing he wouldn't do for Gram, but this…

"I know," his mom said softly, even though he hadn't said anything yet. "But your father and I think she could really get in trouble this time, and unless you can find a loophole in the legal crap your father couldn't, we might have to go along with this scheme she's concocted."

"What exactly are—" He paused. "No, don't tell me. I have a feeling the more I know, the less I'm going to want to show up for it. I'll be at Gram's by ten tomorrow, but I'm not making any promises about staying."

"Thank you, Finn. And Gram said you should bring some old jeans, too. And work boots."

"What?" But his mother, smart woman that she was, had already disconnected.

He dropped his cell phone on his desk and leaned back in his chair. "Unbelievable."

"A few weeks? You've gotta be kidding."

The screen between the two desks didn't offer much in the way of privacy. It existed more to keep him and Tom Brisbin, his business partner, from throwing balled-up paper or shooting rubber bands at each other during working hours.

"It's about Gram," Finn replied. Tom had known his family long enough so he didn't feel a need to say more.

"It always is." A low chuckle filtered through the screen. "I love that woman."

So did Finn, which was the only reason he rolled into Blackberry Bay at ten minutes before ten the following morning. The quaint little town nestled around a bay off Lake Winnipesauke attracted tourists year-round, thanks to their proximity to a popular ski area as well as the water, but summer was their booming season and he had to roll the big Harley-Davidson to a stop at what felt like every crosswalk in town.

He had clothing and toiletry staples in one of the big side bags and what amounted to a mobile office in the other, because he hadn't wanted to pack up his truck and give his family the impression he was on board with an extended stay. After going over the calendar, he and Tom had marked the meetings Finn couldn't miss, but there was no reason he *had* to be in the office otherwise. The day-to-day of their financial management company could be run from practically anywhere, but he didn't want anybody to know that. Especially Gram.

Because three road construction zones in twenty miles had slowed him down, Finn went straight through the intersection with the right turn that would lead to his parents' house, figuring they'd already left, and followed the bay for another mile and a half, until he came to the winding driveway leading up to his grandmother's house.

Finn's grandfather—may he rest in peace— had been one for maintaining appearances, and the outside of the massive Victorian on the hill, overlooking Blackberry Bay, was in pretty good shape, though it was starting to show some wear and tear. The clapboard siding—some original and some not—was painted a muted salmon color and the door and many windows were trimmed in a cream color. It caught the eye without being garish. Blackberry Bay didn't *do* garish.

The two-car garage that had been built to replace a torn-down barn, as well as an original shed that was almost as big as the garage, were painted to match, and if there was one thing Gram could do well, it was tend gardens. From the road, her home was the picture of historical grace and elegance.

Inside, it looked like the seventies and eighties were having an everything-must-go rummage sale.

Or it usually did, anyway. He'd had a busy month at work, so his visits to town had been quick ones, and after visiting his parents, he'd made time for a glass of lemonade with Gram on her front porch. But sometime between his last time inside and today, a whole lot of stuff had been removed and somehow he doubted she'd randomly decided to do a mass decluttering.

"We're in here," his mother called when he gave the front door the extra little shove it needed in order to latch properly behind him.

As if they were ever anywhere but in the kitchen. His footsteps were loud in the foyer as he walked past the doors to the living room and the sitting room—and damn if anybody had ever been able to tell him the difference between the two, other than one having a television and the other having the most uncomfortable wingback chairs he'd ever sat in—to the kitchen.

His parents were seated at the butcher-block table several generations of Weavers had taken their meals around. They were dressed in their usual jeans and T-shirts, though his mom had a lightweight cardigan over hers. They both had short dark hair liberally sprinkled with gray and gave him matching tired smiles.

Gram hopped down from the barstool she'd been sitting on in front of the counter, since the kitchen didn't have a center island. Her gray hair was long and loose around her face, and her white tank top, peach capris and white tennis shoes made him smile as she opened her arms for a hug. Gram refused to age gracefully by seemingly refusing to age at all, thank goodness.

"You made it!" She looked at the clock on the wall and then pinched his arm just hard enough to make him wince. "Barely."

"Hey, barely counts. And of course I made it." He pulled out a seat at the foot of the table and sat. Gram followed suit, sitting across the table from his parents. "So I'm here. Somebody tell me what's going on."

"I have good news!" Gram clapped her hands together one time while his father groaned. "Do you know that show, *Relic Rehab*?"

"Nope."

Her shoulders drooped. "You really should watch more TV, you know. Anyway, they remodel historical homes with businesses in them and they're coming here to remodel the Bayview Inn!"

"Okay." Finn looked from Gram's excited expression to his parents—his mother rolling her eyes and his father shaking his head—and back to Gram. "What's the Bayview Inn?"

"This is." Gram waved her hand in a gesture that encompassed the kitchen before leaning closer. "I've decided I can only afford to keep this place up if I let rich flatlanders—I mean tourists—pay to sleep here, but it needs some updating to be an inn, so I applied to the show and told them it already was. And I got picked!"

"This house has never been an inn and everybody in Blackberry Bay knows it. Everybody in this town knows *everything*."

"I know stuff, too, kiddo. I've lived here my whole life and I know where all the bodies are buried, so you can bet your sweet bippy everybody's going to stick to the script."

Finn groaned and scrubbed a hand over his jaw. "Please tell me you're not blackmailing the neighbors."

"The neighbors? Honey, I'm blackmailing the entire town." She nodded. "The ladies at town hall were going to be a problem, but Jill's mother told Carolina before she passed that Jill got her job because she worked late with one town selectman in particular, if you know what I mean, and his wife's meaner than a badger."

"Gram."

"You sound exactly like your father when you say that." She chuckled. "Except he says 'Mom,' of course. But he makes that same face."

"Mom," his dad said, his voice a groan.

"See?" Gram pointed her finger between the two of them. "Just like that."

"I love you Gram, but this is…" He scrubbed his hand over his face. "Tell her, Dad."

"Trust me, I already have. Several times."

"I don't want to spend the rest of my life trying to scrape up the money to pay taxes on this beast," Gram said, "but I don't want to sell it, either. I don't really have any marketable skills to speak of, but I can do hospitality."

Finn recoiled so hard the old wooden chair creaked under his shifting weight. "You? Hospitable? You chased the plumber out of the house with a broom."

"I wasn't chasing him with the broom. I was trying to hand it to him so he could sweep up the crap he tracked in on his damn boots."

"Mom asked why you had Christmas decorations up the first week of November and you threw her out of the house."

"I like Christmas. And who cares about November? Why do we have to reserve an entire month because we eat turkey on a Thursday?"

"So I guess Thanksgiving dinner isn't a tradition you'll be honoring at the Bayview Inn?"

"Damn. Do people stay at inns for Thanksgiving? They can go eat with whoever they're in town to visit, I guess."

"Gram." He set the lemonade down. "Remember when Mom's parents came to town when Dad proposed to her and you made them stay in a hotel even though you have all these rooms?"

"I remember that, but you don't, since you weren't born yet."

"Even if I have to limit examples of your hospitality to those I actually remember, I can still do this all day."

Gram gave him a that's-enough-out-of-you look and sat back in her chair with her arms folded. "It doesn't matter. It's done. I signed the contract, dealt the cards and now everybody has to play the hands I gave them."

"What exactly is it I'm supposed to be doing?"

"You're the inn's handyman."

He laughed until Miss Hospitality picked up the candle jar in the center of the table and cocked her arm back as if she was going to chuck it at him. "You can't be serious, Gram. Remember when I took shop in high school and the teacher made me switch to home ec because his nerves couldn't handle me being around power tools?"

"Such a proud day for me," his father said in a droll tone.

"Hey, at least I learned how to cook."

"You barely passed that class," his mom pointed out.

His family was so much fun. Really. Finn couldn't imagine why he'd chosen to live an hour away. "At least, unlike in shop class, I couldn't hurt anybody."

His dad groaned. "I don't know. That quiche—"

"You're getting off topic," Gram snapped. "I don't need you to cook. I don't even need you to be particularly handy. I just need you to look like you are."

"What does that even mean?"

"Wear some old jeans and run around with no shirt on. Maybe we should smear some baby oil so you look all hot and sweaty."

"Gram!" He was not letting his grandmother smear him with baby oil. And he never wanted to hear her refer to him as hot and sweaty ever again.

"Simmer down. You can put it on yourself if it makes you feel better."

While doing it himself was certainly a better option than his grandmother doing it, he had no intention of coating his body in fake sweat to appease a camera.

"And do it fast," Gram told him, "because they're going to arrive anytime now."

"Well, this is certainly quaint."

Anna Beckett tore her gaze from the rural scenery passing outside the window to look over at her assistant. They would both consider themselves city girls if asked, but where Anna was entranced by the woods and the charming homes and the glimpses of a lake, Eryn Landsperger's voice was droll.

"No more than the last town," Anna said.

Eryn shook her head, her blond ponytail swinging. "This one feels different."

Turning back to her window, Anna shivered. *This one feels different.* Because this town *was* different, though she was absolutely the only person who knew why. And she intended to keep it that way.

"Home sweet home for the next six to eight weeks," Eryn said, and then she sighed. "Or more, probably."

The Bayview Inn was going to be their anchor project—the two-part finale that would wrap up a season of smaller projects, even though it was filmed first to take advantage of as much of a guarantee of good weather that New England offered. The final projects were always the biggest of the year in terms of cost, square footage and historical value.

The Bayview Inn only checked off two of those boxes, and the old Victorian in Blackberry Bay would definitely be Anna's most challenging project ever. It had been since the day they met to go through the latest crop of applications submitted through the website and she'd seen the name of the town. The team had dismissed the application because the paperwork proving the provenance of the inn was sparse, but she'd made a joke about how small towns didn't always do things the way they were supposed to and urged them to focus on the beautiful old house.

And she hammered home the fact that according to Tess's application, her son and his wife, as well as her grandson, lived locally and would be part of the renovation. While their project owners varied, the ratings were always highest when there was a family group involved with the filming.

The Bayview Inn was a project she really wanted—a fact she'd made known to executive producer Duncan Forrest, though she hadn't told him why. If she played her cards right, nobody from the show ever needed to know she'd taken on this project for personal reasons.

"We're running late," Eryn said after checking the time on her smartwatch. They always allowed for traffic, but nobody could predict a truck hauling a fifth-wheel trailer rolling and ending up across all three lanes of traffic in southern New Hampshire. "We'll barely have time to park the RVs and get to the inn, never mind getting them set up and exploring the town."

"The town's been here over two hundred and fifty years. It'll probably still be here after we meet Mrs. Weaver and see the inn." She snorted when Eryn rapped her knuckles on the fake wood door trim. "But you're right. We'll definitely have to dump the RVs and run."

When the drivers pulled the RVs into the lake-front campground they'd be calling home for a while, Anna wished she had the time to explore, but as soon as they got the compact car unhooked from its tow bar, she and Eryn had to go. They'd leave the large SUV driven by Mike, the senior cameraman, at the end of the convoy of vehicles for the crew to use.

They had no trouble finding the house, and while she was familiar with it thanks to the extensive video and numerous photos she'd reviewed, she always felt a rush of anticipation when she first set eyes on a new project.

An elderly woman wearing a floral dress and an apron opened the front door for them. After giving them a huge smile, she stepped back and welcomed them in with a theatrical sweep of her arm. "Welcome to the Bayview Inn. I'm your hostess, Tess Weaver."

"I'm Anna," she managed to say with a straight face. If she hadn't already guessed Tess's story was largely fabricated, the exaggerated performance would have tipped her off. "And this is my assistant, Eryn. We're so excited to be here, Mrs. Weaver."

"I'm excited to have you here. Do you want a tour?"

"Honestly, I'd rather just sit and talk to you for a few minutes," Anna replied. "We watched the video tour several times, and we've been traveling all morning, so the rest of production is busy right now, setting up."

"Come into the kitchen and I'll get you some lemonade."

She saw Eryn's wince and knew the first thing they did after leaving here would be finding a local coffee shop. "Actually, we'd love some water if you don't mind."

While Tess poured them each a glass of ice water, Anna looked over the kitchen. The place was definitely overdue for a renovation. By several decades.

"How did the town get its name?" she asked, taking the glass she was offered. She found small talk about familiar subjects put people at ease faster than jumping right into production talk.

Tess chuckled. "It's quite a story."

"We love to sprinkle local flavor throughout the episodes, so I'm always up for a good story."

"Well, as legend has it, the founders of Blackberry Bay were exploring the area and they found this beautiful bay off the big lake, and the entire area had been overrun by wild blackberry bushes."

After a few seconds of silence, Anna realized that was the entirety of the story, but she couldn't tell by Tess's expression if she was trying to be funny or if she really believed that was *quite a story*. Anna didn't bother to ask how the Bayview Inn got its name. Being literal seemed to be a theme around here. "I guess we should all be thankful it wasn't overrun by poison ivy, then."

Tess's laugh covered Eryn's groan, and Anna smiled. "So your application essay said your husband passed away and business has declined due to guests choosing more updated lodging. And you've been running the inn by yourself?"

"For the most part. My son and his wife disappeared somewhere, unfortunately, but let me introduce you to my grandson. He's such a good boy, doing his best to take care of me and this old house...inn. Taking care of his grandma and this inn. Finn, honey," she said to somebody behind Anna, "come say hello."

Anna turned, expecting to see a young man—

maybe even a teenager—blushing awkwardly at his grandmother's praise.

The man was not a teenager and there was nothing awkward about him. And she could only hope *she* wasn't blushing when he put out his hand for her to shake.

"Finn Weaver," he said in a voice she might have been tempted to pay $2.99 per minute to hear saying naughty things over the phone.

He was tall, with short brown hair shot through with natural highlights, and dark eyes that looked at her intently as she shook his hand. The jeans that were so soft and well-worn they practically hugged his body and the tight navy T-shirt fit the job description, but as she shook his hand, something felt not quite right.

This guy was who Tess was passing off as her handyman? The softness of his hands and the well-kept nails would explain the sorry condition of the inn—if it actually was one. Hell, she probably had more calluses than he did, and she didn't skimp on hand lotion.

She might have her doubts about him doing physical labor, but it was obvious he was no stranger to working out. In a gym. Probably an expensive one, too. There was just something about his strong body and impeccable grooming that smacked of money. Finn Weaver looked like a high-maintenance kind of man.

Anna did her best to focus on Tess's chatter—she was talking about her ancestors now, or maybe her husband's—but Finn moving around the kitchen and pouring himself a glass of lemonade was distracting her. He not only looked good, but he smelled good, too. Even his scent was tantalizing and expensive.

She wasn't sure exactly what was going on in the Bayview Inn, but she knew one thing for sure. Anna and Tess weren't the only people in the room who were hiding something.

Chapter Two

Finn hadn't had time between being informed of Gram's plan and this moment to run a Google search on *Relic Rehab*, so he'd been expecting a couple of guys in fake work clothes—the designer label T-shirts and jeans sprinkled with a little Sheetrock dust.

"I'm Anna Beckett, the host of *Relic Rehab*," the woman had told him as he'd somewhat reluctantly released her hand.

The stunning brunette with the big, dark eyes and warm smile threw him for a loop. She was wearing navy capri pants and a navy-and-white striped top with a wide neck that made him want to hook his finger under it and stroke her collarbone.

It had been a long time since he'd felt an instant attraction this potent, and of course it had to be for a woman he absolutely, under no circumstances, could make a pass at. Not when he was lying to her and she held his grandmother's financial welfare in her hands.

He couldn't let his guard down for even a moment when it came to remembering Anna was very much off-limits to him.

"It's nice to meet you," he had said in as casual a voice as he could muster.

"It's nice to meet you, too," she'd responded, looking him in the eye.

Now Anna's gaze locked with his again for a few seconds, and then she glanced at her smartwatch before smiling at Gram. "The crew is here, so Eryn and I are going to go meet them so we can look around and figure out where we want to start, if you don't mind."

Finn tried not to watch her leave, but he couldn't stop himself. She was talking to her assistant, who punctuated everything her boss said with a sharp nod, and he liked the way Anna's entire body seemed to move with purpose. *A real firecracker*, his grandfather would have said.

Then he looked—*really* looked—at his grandmother and thoughts of the unexpectedly sexy show host flew out of his mind. Apparently she'd taken the time before the crew's arrival to change her clothes. And her hair. And pretty much everything. "Gram, what is wrong with you?"

"Not a darn thing. What's wrong with *you*?"

"Why do you look like…that?" He waved a hand over her, from her hair put up in a bun to the polyester pants to the orthopedic sneakers on her feet. And she was bent over a little, one hand on her hip. "And why are you walking like that? Did you hurt yourself?"

"Lower your voice," she said in a hard whisper. "I'm fine. I did it for the application video so they'd take pity on an old widow, so now I have to keep doing it."

Finn sighed and dropped his head. A few seconds with his eyes closed didn't do a lot to center him, though, and he wasn't sure if he was mad at her or about to laugh.

When it came to Gram, the answer was usually a little of both.

"There's no way you're going to be able to do this for weeks," he told her. "Not only do you have the energy of a six-month-old puppy, but walking like that is going to make your muscles sore. Or worse."

"Don't worry about me, Finn. You just focus on looking handy. And hush now, because they're coming back."

He'd always been a social drinker at best, but right now Finn was sorely tempted to hide in the barn with one of the bottles of bourbon very few people knew his grandfather had kept in a wooden crate bearing the logo of a motor oil company that had gone out of business decades ago. His grandfather's stinginess with money had extended to his liquor, so the surviving bottles might lose in a blind taste test to turpentine, but he'd probably have a better chance of getting through this if he wasn't entirely sober.

On the other hand, he thought as Anna and one of the cameramen rounded the corner, having his wits about him might not be a bad thing as long as this woman was here. There was something about her that made him feel like an awkward teenage boy again, and he couldn't take the chance of stupid crap flying out of his mouth as it had when he'd actually been that age.

"Your electrical system isn't in bad shape," Anna said to Gram when she reached them. "Quite a bit of it's been updated, so we have more outlets than we're used to finding in old homes like this."

"One of my oldest friends is an electrician," Finn told her, drawing those pretty eyes his way again. "Gram has an affinity for extension cords older than me and he's rather fond of her, so he's done some work around the place to keep her from accidentally burning it down."

"Would have been nice if you were friends with a plumber and an HVAC guy, too," Gram muttered.

"Or a family therapist," he muttered back.

"Well, we're here now," Anna said in a chipper voice. "We're not only going to help you restore the Bayview Inn to her former glory, but bring her up to code, too. Tess, Eryn's in the living room working on my introduction. She's hoping you might have a few minutes to confirm the details about the inn that she's included."

"Sure thing," Gram said before hobbling out of the room. It took everything Finn had not to roll his eyes.

"I'll go get set up so we can do a run-through for the opening walk-and-talk," the cameraman said.

Anna nodded and the guy walked away, leaving them alone in the room. When Finn gave her a questioning look, she smiled. "It's literally what it sounds like. They're going to film me walking toward the camera while I give a quick intro about the house in the background."

"Tough job."

"It's not as easy as it sounds, you know."

He liked the way the tops of her cheeks and that little patch of skin just above her top button turned a light pink when she was annoyed. "You might want to hurry, since it's going to rain soon."

"Oh, really?" She arched her eyebrow and the look she gave him was pure snark. "Can you smell it in the air? Feel an ache in your bones?"

He had an ache in his bone all right, but it had nothing to do with the impending rain. "I watched the weather forecast this morning."

"Oh." She chuckled, and then, after a glance at her watch, rolled her eyes. "And, of course, there's my notification that precipitation will be starting soon."

"I'll get out of your way, then."

"You're free to watch, if you want, but I should warn you that this part's pretty boring."

"I doubt that." He was pretty confident that watching Anna Beckett work would be anything *but* boring.

Anna very rarely flubbed a line, especially in the opening walk-and-talk when walking in a straight line and introducing the project were literally *all* she had to do, but she was on her fourth take and even Eryn was beginning to look concerned.

"It's Bayview, not Bayside," her assistant reminded her for the second time, making Anna wish that Tess had kept it simple while coming up with a name for her fake inn. The Weaver Inn would have been easier to remember.

She nodded at Eryn, but all the reminders in the world weren't going to help as long as Finn Weaver was leaned up against a tree, arms folded across his chest, watching her. She'd meant it when she told him he was welcome to watch, but she hadn't anticipated how much trouble she was going to have concentrating while his gaze was following her every step.

She was a professional, dammit. And even if she'd engineered this visit to Blackberry Bay under slightly sketchy circumstances, this was her job and she was good at it. Usually.

It didn't matter if Finn was watching her. Or that she *liked* that he wanted to watch her. What mattered was producing a great show for her viewers and, during her downtime, finding answers to the questions that had been haunting her since her parents divorced when she was sixteen and she found out the woman she believed was her mother was, in fact, her stepmother.

"Anna, do you need a minute?"

Eryn's concern cut through the turmoil in her head and Anna nodded. "Yeah. Sorry, but I need a quick break."

She'd known coming to this town would be hard, but she'd foolishly believed she could keep the two reasons for being in Blackberry Bay separated. One was business. One was personal. But they were so intertwined she wasn't going to be able to compartmentalize. And the enormity of what she was doing in this town was starting to hit her and it couldn't have picked a worse time.

"I am literally watching the clouds roll in right

now," Mike said. He was not only the senior of the two cameramen, but he'd been with her since the very beginning, when it was just the two of them making their own show for YouTube. He was never shy about speaking up.

"It's just a run-through," Eryn replied, her voice a little sharp. "It's not that big a deal if we don't get it today."

It was a little bit of a big deal, Anna thought, since they always filmed the walk-and-talk first, to get it out of the way. Especially if they were going to do any construction on the exterior of the property. Mike liked to do a full practice run-through so he could check the angles and make any adjustments that might be needed. The inn's front lawn and walkway had a slight downward slope to it, and until Anna got through the entire opening bit, he wouldn't know if he needed to elevate the camera to compensate. It also let him ensure nothing got into the periphery of the shot, like a lawn mower or a stray garbage bin. It was a lot easier to get it done before they started tearing a property apart.

"One more minute," she told Mike, and then she closed her eyes and took a few deep breaths.

"Are you sure you're okay?" Eryn asked in a low voice meant only for her ears.

Anna nodded but didn't open her eyes. Even though this project had been in the planning stages for a while, it had been just theoretical. But the familiar physical action of filming the opening walk-and-talk had triggered the awareness this was very, very real. It was happening.

She was going to be in Blackberry Bay for weeks, helping the Weaver family renovate their historic inn and looking for more information about her birth mother.

It was a lot.

But after one more deep breath, she opened her eyes and looked Eryn in the eye. She could do this. "I'm okay. I'm ready."

As she turned back toward Mike, she saw that Finn was gone. On the one hand, that was a good thing. Having him around probably wasn't great for her ability to focus on what she was doing. But there was a part of her that wished he'd stayed long enough to see her actually nail the walk-and-talk run-through like the professional she was.

Twenty minutes later, Mike had the minimum he needed and they were all in the house, hiding from the heavy rain. Tess had put out baked goods and beverages, so everybody was in a pretty good mood.

She also got the opportunity to meet Tess's son Joel and his wife, Alice. Joel looked like an older, softer version of his son, though Finn definitely had Alice's eyes. The couple smiled and said all the right words, but it was fairly obvious neither of them wanted to be there. And based on the looks

Alice kept tossing her mother-in-law's way, they probably hadn't been brought into Tess's fraud until it was too late to do anything but go along with it.

Maybe it was just because she was inexplicably drawn to Finn, but she hoped the same was true for him. She preferred to think he'd gotten sucked into his grandmother's plan as opposed to being a willing accomplice.

After a while, she snuck out of the kitchen everybody was gathered in and made her way to the front porch. Sinking into an old wicker rocker, she let the cool breeze wash over her while she watched the rain falling.

On the far side of the road at the bottom of the drive was a stand of trees, and beyond that she could see the gray expanse of Blackberry Bay. On a clear, sunny day, it must be a stunning view, she thought. Or in the fall, when the trees and rolling hills around the lake were a blaze of yellow, orange and red.

"Mind if I join you?" a deep voice asked, and Anna's skin tingled at the sound of it.

"Of course not. It's your porch."

He sat in a rocker that matched hers, on the other side of the door, so she'd actually have to turn her head to see him. That was okay with her, because the voice was bad enough. The voice and the face together might make her say something stupid.

"Are you really going to film us moving Gram's stuff out of here tomorrow?" he asked after the silence had drawn on for a few minutes.

She chuckled. "Just a little bit of it, for color. As you know, we had a crew come out last week and move most of the big stuff into the storage pods, but one of the things viewers like about *Relic Rehab*'s do-it-yourself vibe is the excitement. You can watch a hundred different shows about replacing bathroom tile or maximizing a home's footprint, but our viewers want the *story*. Not only the story of the property, but of the people who care enough to preserve it for the future."

"Yeah, it's quite a story," Finn muttered, and Anna had to bite back her laugh. She wasn't supposed to know just what a tall tale Tess Weaver was spinning.

This project was definitely going to keep her on her toes. She'd already had to deal with comments from the crew who'd moved stuff into the pods. The extra rooms in the house hadn't exactly looked like the kind of rooms people paying to vacation by a lake would pay to sleep in. But she'd waved it off and said some people preferred simple. There were probably going to be hundreds of opportunities for her or for the Weavers to slip up, and she needed to pay attention at all times.

Then she heard the creak of wicker as he leaned back in the rocker, and a male sigh of contentment that made her toes curl in her tennis shoes. Daring to turn her head, she watched him rocking slowly, his mouth curled into a small smile as he looked out over the bay.

The shiver of desire made her turn her gaze back to the water in a hurry. "It's so peaceful out here."

"Most of the time," he said softly. "My family can be loud, but I guess you'll find that out yourself. I mean, don't get me wrong. It's all love. But it gets loud, and my mom and Gram can push each other's buttons like nobody's business."

"It sounds like you're trying to warn me, but I have to confess that a loving but loud family doing a renovation together makes for great television." She leaned her head back and rocked her chair in time with his. That was her hope for the Weavers— that the episodes would be so engaging the network wouldn't care if they discovered the truth behind her acceptance of Tess's questionable application. "The fun really starts tomorrow."

"I can't wait," he replied without an ounce of sincerity.

Chuckling softly, she watched the rain fall and tried to convince that panicky voice inside her head that, no, she had *not* gotten herself in over her head here.

She was almost sure of it.

Chapter Three

Wet, sloppy kisses to the face weren't always a bad way to wake up, but Finn could have done without the cairn terrier morning breath.

"Grizz, get off me." The dog yipped and tried to stick his tongue in Finn's ear. "Okay, now you're just making it weird."

He used both hands to scratch Grizzly's neck, which not only made the dog's whole body tremble with glee but enabled Finn to hold the doggy kisses at bay. It was his own fault for not making sure his bedroom door had latched before he crawled into bed. The house he'd grown up in wasn't as old as Gram's house, but it was old enough that a door being closed and a door being completely latched so a small but determined dog couldn't push it open were two different things.

"I'd say you have some massively bad bed head, but you always look like this, don't you?" Finn tried to smooth down the dog's brindle coat, with its dark blend of grays, browns and reds. No matter how often they groomed him, he always looked like he'd come straight from licking a light socket.

Most of the time, he acted like it, too.

Finn's phone chimed with a message, and when he reached to the nightstand for it, Grizz took the opportunity to pounce on his head as if it had been years since he'd seen Finn and not a few weeks.

Breakfast is ready.

"It must be a special occasion, Grizz." His mom didn't mind cooking supper most nights, but her breakfast style had always run more toward pointing in the direction of the cereal cabinet.

Then he remembered. Today was officially Day One of Gram's newest escapade, and the timing couldn't have been worse.

It was moving-out day, so of course it was going to be an unseasonably hot and humid one. By the time he was done hauling the rest of Gram's crap to the storage pods the production crew had hidden in a part of the yard that couldn't be seen in a wide shot of the house, he wouldn't need baby oil to look sweaty. He was just thankful they'd already taken care of the heavy stuff.

"We have to get up," he told the dog, who ignored him. "Grizz, you want some bacon?"

The dog was practically a blur as he took off toward the kitchen. If his mom hadn't made bacon, Finn was really going to feel like a jerk.

Luckily, as soon as he was dressed and hit the top of the stairs, Finn could smell bacon. And coffee. His stomach growled just as he stepped into the kitchen and his mom swiveled to face him, hands on her hips.

"Did you promise this dog bacon?"

"Guilty." When she scowled, he held up his hands. "It's the only way he'd let me get out of bed."

"He weighs fourteen pounds."

"But a very stubborn fourteen pounds." He kissed his mother's cheek and poured himself a cup of coffee before sitting at the table. "Morning, Dad."

"Morning. He's getting one of your slices."

"Fair." After serving himself from the bowl of scrambled eggs and grabbing toast and bacon from their serving plates, he broke a bacon slice into a bunch of small pieces. If he rationed it out correctly, he could get through his breakfast without having to sacrifice a second slice to the dog.

"You know how much I love when you two feed

the dog from the table," his mom said, but there was enough affection in her voice so Finn didn't worry too much about it.

"Dad started it," he said. "Sneaking him french fries when Grizz was a pup."

His dad set his coffee cup down with a thump. "Do you have a license to drive that bus?"

"He's hardly throwing you under the bus, Joel. It's not like I wasn't there the first time you snuck him food under the table. Or every single time since."

Winking at him over a slice of toast, his dad shrugged. "How do you tell that face no?"

"I manage."

Finn laughed. "You say no, but it's kind of funny what a hard time you have getting tater tots from your fork to your mouth. You *accidentally* drop as many as you eat."

She opened her mouth, as if to deny it, and then snapped it closed again. Her pink cheeks made it clear enough she knew this was a rare argument she couldn't win.

When breakfast was over, Finn and his dad cleared the table and loaded the dishwasher. A best-of-three round of Rock, Paper, Scissors had Dad stuck with cleaning Mom's beloved cast-iron pan to her exacting standards, which was a relief. Finn still cringed when he thought of The Awful Scouring Pad Incident of 2002.

Eventually the clock caught up with him and he couldn't put it off anymore. "Time to grab my boots and my work gloves, I guess. I still can't believe I got sucked into this."

"We," his mother snapped, giving his dad a look that made it clear their current predicament was entirely his fault because it was his mother who'd gotten them into it. "Somehow your father and I got added into the mix and we're supposed to be there, too."

"Apparently loving but loud families make for great television, according to Anna," Finn said, and he wasn't surprised when his mother rolled her eyes. "Don't forget the loving part, okay?"

"You know I love your grandmother, but sometimes…"

She never finished those sentences which, all things considered, was probably for the best. "What are we going to do with Grizz?"

"I don't know how they'll feel about a dog on the set," his dad said.

"It's not a damn set," his mother muttered, not quite under her breath.

"Close enough, since anywhere my mother is standing seems to become a stage."

"People will be in and out of the house, carrying things," Finn said. "Grizz underfoot is just a disaster waiting to happen."

"Since your grandmother is also a disaster waiting to happen, her and Grizz both being there would probably be an apocalypse in the making," his mother said. "I'll ask Libby to watch him for today, while we see how it goes."

Even if their neighbor dog-sat for them—which she did fairly often—it was going to be a very long day. His mother usually called Gram by her name and occasionally even *Mom*, but when she called her *your mother* or *your grandmother*, sparks were inevitably going to fly.

Hopefully, having the camera around would keep the worst of it at bay. Yes, the entire family was annoyed with Gram at the moment. Yes, his mother and grandmother tended to butt heads at times. But when push came to shove, there was nothing she wouldn't do for her mother-in-law, and Finn was confident that included going along with the current shenanigans. Mostly confident. Fairly.

It was going to be a very long day.

The first full day on location was always one of Anna's least favorites, and it had a lot to do with having spent the night trying to readjust to sleeping in the RV after a long break in filming.

She'd replaced the stock camper mattress with a real mattress when they bought it, but it still wasn't her bed. And she lived alone. Though Eryn slept in the bunk over the cab at the other end, that was only twenty-six feet away or so, and Anna felt as though she woke up every time Eryn moved.

The adjustment wouldn't take long. She knew from experience that busy days would have her accustomed to RV living and sleeping through the night in no time. The first morning was always the hardest.

"Coffee's ready," Eryn called, and Anna threw back the blankets.

Coffee always helped.

Thirty minutes later, she was on her second cup and almost ready to face the day. There were granola bars and bananas for breakfast, but she skipped those for now. There was a wider variety of foods in the other RV because it had a bigger fridge, and she'd probably grab something from it later.

"So…" Eryn said, propping her elbows on the small dinette table. "Chemistry much?"

Anna nodded. "Yeah, the Weaver family's going to play well on TV, for sure."

"Cool, but I meant you and the handyman grandson."

"Finn?"

"Yes, Finn. There was so much sizzle in the room I thought their antique electrical panel was finally shorting out."

"You're imagining things," Anna replied, but she could feel the heat spreading across her skin.

"You know, if we hurry, we can stop and explore the town a little before we head to the inn. Maybe pick up some pastries or something."

"You're trying to change the subject."

"Fine. We can sit here and discuss your delusions, and we'll go straight to the house. No pastries."

Eryn's eyes narrowed. "You're a pretty evil boss. I'll be ready to leave in ten minutes."

It was slightly cool when they stepped outside, but Anna had checked the forecast and knew today was going to be a scorcher.

The motor homes blended in with the assortment of RVs parked around them in the waterfront campground. Their first RV had been wrapped with a huge *Relic Rehab* advertisement and they couldn't say if it had gained them any new viewers, but they were pretty confident it was the reason somebody had broken into it and stolen their equipment.

Now they had two motor homes—one for Anna and Eryn, and one for the guys—and they didn't give any indication there might be anything more than vacation brochures and s'mores sticks inside. Nor had they put the show's name on the side of the trailer towed behind the crew's SUV. The tools inside were worth almost as much as the AV equipment in the SUV that pulled it, and they'd all be relieved when it was moved to the Weaver property today.

Anna drove so Eryn could review the task list for the day, but it was a short drive from the campground to the municipal free parking lot, so she finished while they walked the main street. Being able to read her phone, walk and talk at the same time was one of Eryn's most finely honed skills.

"I think we need to keep Alice and Tess in close proximity," Anna added when she was done. "They're oil and water, but there's obviously genuine affection there, so we'll get some good footage—oh, you have got to be kidding me."

Eryn looked up from her phone when Anna stopped walking. "What?"

She pointed at the sign across the street proclaiming in block letters that the cream-colored building with the pretty blue trim and attached brick garage was the home of Bishop's Auto Care and Bakery.

"Cars and cupcakes," Eryn said. "I love this town."

"They could have separate signs. Just to... I don't know. Not be a combination auto repair and baked goods shop?"

"Since the apostrophe is before the *s*, there's only one Bishop, though."

"Or maybe the owner sucks at grammar."

Eryn nodded. "That's a strong possibility, since

people who suck at grammar always put the apostrophe before the *s*."

"Probably should have gone with separate signs, though."

"Look at those cupcakes in the window. We *have* to go in." Eryn was already heading for the crosswalk.

"We don't need auto care *or* cupcakes," Anna pointed out, but she followed her anyway.

"You said we'd get pastries."

"I meant an apple strudel, or some other at least vaguely breakfast-related pastry."

"Who says cupcakes aren't vaguely breakfast-related? Or we can get some now and save them for later."

Anna considered that. "But if we save them for later, we have to buy enough for everybody because we can't leave them sitting in the car all day."

"We can get one and split it now," Eryn suggested, ever the problem solver.

As soon as she stepped through the door of the bakery, Anna was pretty sure she gained five pounds just from breathing in the aroma. The shop smelled like carbs and calories.

A woman paused halfway through frosting a cupcake to give them a welcoming smile. "Good morning, ladies. Feel free to look at the selection and let me know if you have any questions. I'm Jenelle."

"Thank you." Anna wasn't sure how they were going to be able to choose just one. And the more they looked, the harder the decision got.

"Hey, Mom, do you think you can watch Parker this afternoon so I can get this exhaust done? Mrs. Cloutier broke a crown and she doesn't want to take him to the dentist with her." A redhead wearing coveralls with *Reyna* stitched on the breast pocket came through a rear door, and then stopped short. "Sorry. Didn't realize you had customers."

"Don't mind us," Anna said. "It's going to take us five or six hours to decide."

"I'm always available to watch my grandson," Jenelle said.

"Oh, so mother-and-daughter businesses," Anna said. "Auto care and bakery."

"That makes sense," Eryn added. "Still, two Bishops, though."

"The apostrophe?" Reyna asked, and when they both nodded, she laughed. "If you look closely, you can see the *and bakery* part was added later. There used to be only one Bishop—my dad—but now it's mine, and my mom opened the bakery and…hey, why spend money you don't have to?"

Her mother chuckled. "Plus we'd miss out on all the visitors who feel compelled to check out a place that offers auto care *and* cupcakes."

"If I lived in this town, I'd have my oil changed

every five hundred miles," Eryn confessed. "But for now, I'm only going to choose one cupcake."

"*We're* only choosing one," Anna reminded her. "We're splitting one. For now. But we'll definitely be back."

"If you're only having one, I recommend the blackberry cream cupcake with the vanilla bean buttercream frosting," Reyna said. "I have to get to work, but it was nice to meet you. Good luck with Tess."

Anna looked at her—perhaps more sharply than she'd intended—because they hadn't told the woman who they were and she wasn't sure she wanted Tess brought into the conversation while Eryn was standing right next to her.

Reyna must have mistaken her look for being caught off guard at being recognized. "I've seen your show a few times. And my husband and I didn't hear about you coming to town until yesterday, but Tess must be excited."

"She is. And we're excited to get started."

After Reyna left, Anna tried to pay attention to Eryn running through their cupcake choices, but she was still thinking about the fact an entire town knew that Tess Weaver's house hadn't been an inn for very long, if ever. While Anna might have indulged in some fast, excited chatter about the house to keep the production from digging too deep into the application, she'd done a deeper dive on her own and confirmed her suspicion: Blackberry Bay had never had a Bayview Inn.

The few official documents Tess had provided had obviously been doctored. A slightly different font that was only noticeable if a person zoomed in on the PDF files. A document written in an old handwritten script that had obviously been pieced together by taking phrases and words from other documents. While it was a step above the look of a ransom note, it was a short step, and Anna was glad taking possession of the applications to study was part of her usual process. She didn't want anybody else from *Relic Rehab* taking a closer look at them.

But was Tess Weaver really so beloved in Blackberry Bay that the entire town was willing to cover for her? Anna hoped so.

When she and Eryn finally decided to take Reyna's advice because she would know the best flavors, after all, Jenelle sliced the cupcake neatly in half before putting it into a small box.

"I actually brought cash with me," Eryn said. "I don't usually carry cash, but I wasn't sure if, you know…"

Anna winced as Eryn trailed off before she could make it worse, but the woman only laughed. "Even in Blackberry Bay, it's 2020. This town runs on tourism and tourists want it to look quaint, but they also expect to pay for things with a wave of their watches and have free Wi-Fi for their kids."

After Anna paid with a wave of her watch, they thanked Jenelle and continued their walk. The sun had already burned off the slight morning chill, and she knew once the humidity started building, it was going to get uncomfortable fast. They sat in the shade of a gazebo on the town square to eat the cupcake—which was as delicious as Reyna had promised—and then started walking back in the direction of the municipal lot.

Eryn stopped under a sign that said BLACK-BERRY BAY MARKET in block letters, with An Old-Fashioned General Store written underneath in a smaller script. "We need to remember this place to come back to later so we can stock up on something other than granola bars."

"Let's just check it out really quick right now, because if we have to find a bigger store or even drive out of town to do grocery shopping, the sooner we know, the better. We can start a running list."

Eryn laughed. "You say that as if we don't come up with the same list every jobsite and I don't keep a copy on my phone to save time."

But she climbed the wooden stairs and pulled open the screen door. Anna followed her in, surprised there were so many customers at this time of day. The store was a clean, well-lit and organized blend of small grocery store and—as advertised—an old-fashioned general store. There were plenty of souvenirs and handcrafted goods for the tourists, but as they explored the aisles, she was pleased to see the shelves were stocked with a variety of staples.

A strangled squeaking sound behind her made Anna turn suddenly, her body tensing.

Eryn was the source of the sound, but Anna didn't see an obvious reason for the distressed squeak. "What's wrong?"

"Do you see that? What *is* that?"

Anna realized she was talking about the very large and expertly taxidermied moose in the back of the store and struggled not to laugh outright at her friend. "Are you talking about the moose?"

"*That's* a moose?"

"How have you never seen a moose before?"

Eryn glared at her. "I've seen pictures of them. I just thought they were more like goofy deer than goofy *giant* horses."

"Television? Movies?"

"I guess I don't watch a lot of moose-related shows, Anna."

"His name's Morris." They both jumped at the sound of a male voice right behind them. "He's a big one, all right."

They turned to face an older man who, if Anna

had to guess, probably played the town Santa Claus every year.

"If you need anything, just holler. I'm Bob, by the way." He was smiling, but then his gaze narrowed on Anna and he tilted his head. "Have we met before?"

She gave him the friendly—but not *too* friendly—smile she'd practiced in a mirror when people first started recognizing her in public. It didn't happen often because, let's face it, remodeling shows weren't the same as blockbuster movies, but after the second awkward moment of recognition, she'd decided to rehearse her response until it felt natural to her.

"I don't think we have," she said in a chipper voice before shifting the conversation away from herself. "So, uh…did you shoot the moose yourself?"

"Nope. He came already stuffed from a guy over in Maine because tourists love seeing a moose, even if it's dead. Moms love taking their kids' pictures with Morris, let me tell you. He's quite popular with the girls and their selfies, too."

Anna hadn't missed the fact the shelves near the moose were lined with toys and junk food, but she didn't congratulate him on the marketing win. "I'm sure he is."

"Are you sure we haven't met? I'm positive I

know you from somewhere, but I can't place from where."

"I'm sure. But I get that a lot because I'm on TV, on a show called *Relic Rehab*. People who don't watch it still see commercials and ads on the internet, so there's a vague sense of familiarity."

"Maybe. I don't watch a lot of television except for that one station that plays all the *Gunsmoke* repeats."

"So do you own the store?" Eryn asked, and Anna imagined they were about to hear about how his great-grandpa opened the first store in town and it had passed down from generation to generation.

"Oh, I don't own it." He nodded toward the back of the store. "Sydney does."

Anna took a step forward and peered down the aisle. A Black woman about her own age saw her and waved. Then she set whatever she'd been looking at back on the shelf and headed toward them.

"Good afternoon," she said. "Is there something in particular you're looking for?"

Bob answered before Anna could. "She asked me if I owned the store and I was just telling them you're the owner. I help out during tourist season because I get on my wife's nerves when I'm underfoot."

"You know I can't do it without you, Bob." Facing Anna, she held out her hand. "Sydney Ames."

"Anna Beckett, and this is my friend Eryn Landsperger." When they weren't meeting people in a professional capacity, she always introduced Eryn as her friend, rather than her assistant. Not only was it less awkward for everybody, but she and Eryn actually had developed a friendship over the last few years.

"How long have you been in Blackberry Bay?"

"Today's our first full day," Eryn said. "It's a beautiful town."

"We have some amazing postcards made by local artists if you'd like to rub your vacation in the face of those few friends and family members who refuse to get Facebook or Instagram."

Anna laughed. "I'll definitely check them out, even though we're not really on vacation. We're in town to help renovate the Bayview Inn."

"The what?" Bob looked confused.

So did Sydney for a few seconds, and then she smiled and gave Bob what she probably thought was a subtle poke with her elbow. "The Bayview Inn! That's right. Remember, Bob, that a TV show is coming to help Tess renovate her *inn*?"

"Right." He nodded, though he still looked a little confused, in Anna's opinion.

And that wasn't good because Eryn was sharp, and if she caught on that something was amiss, the game could be over before Anna even got to play a hand.

She made a show out of checking the time on her smartwatch. "We really need to run if we don't want to be late. It was nice to meet you, Sydney. Bob. I'm sure you'll be seeing a lot of us while we're here."

After getting Eryn out of the market without Bob letting the cat out of the bag, Anna breathed a sigh of relief. But she also knew this was only the first day. The more time Eryn and the rest of the crew spent in town, the higher the chances they'd find out the Bayview Inn didn't exist.

When Eryn pulled into Tess's driveway, though, seeing the black Harley-Davidson parked next to Tess's car drove the worries about being exposed right out of her head.

Right now, she needed to focus all of her attention on pretending she wasn't attracted to the very hot grandson pretending to be the handyman.

Chapter Four

Anna had already guessed the Weaver family was going to make for interesting television, but she'd had no idea just how much of a handful they were going to be until she had them all together in the kitchen and was trying to give them a brief overview of what was expected of them.

As soon as Tess walked into the kitchen, wearing some kind of floral caftan with orthopedic sneakers, her daughter-in-law had groaned and looked up at the ceiling as if seeking divine guidance. Joel sat at the table, looking at neither his wife nor his mother but at the tabletop, since that was probably all he could see while he was clutching his head in his hands.

Anna could handle all of that. Families who renovated together tended to get on each other's nerves pretty quickly. But Finn? She wasn't sure she could handle him.

He was leaning against the wall, his arms folded over his chest, which just drew her attention to the way his biceps looked in the snug T-shirt. And unlike the other members of the Weaver family, he looked slightly amused by the goings-on. As a matter of fact, when his grandmother had entered the kitchen, it looked as though he'd been fighting back an urge to laugh, but she wasn't sure what to make of that.

It was pretty clear Joel and Alice wanted nothing to do with Tess's plan to get a free renovation from Anna's show, but she couldn't really decipher where Finn stood on the idea. The one time their gazes had locked across the kitchen, there'd been a whole lot of sizzle, but no answers.

"Do you all have smartphones?" Eryn asked after a glance at her phone, which was where all of her lists lived.

"I don't." Tess pointed at what looked like an antique flip phone sitting on the counter. "Mine's a *not-smart* phone. It's probably dead, though, because I lost the charger cord."

"When did you last charge it?" Alice asked.

"I know I used the cell phone to call Jenelle

when Reyna had her baby, because I was at the market when I heard."

"Parker's ten months old, Mom," Joel said, and the low growling sound Alice made in her throat was a signal to Anna that she needed to keep this meeting moving.

She cleared her throat to get everybody's attention back to her. "Because *Relic Rehab* was a You-Tube hit before the network ever picked it up, my audience really enjoys the candid moments caught on cell phone video. We'll have Tess covered, but the rest of you should feel free to video anything you might think is fun or interesting, especially interaction between you, and we'll review it for inclusion if you sign releases for it."

"Do we get paid what your cameramen get paid?" Joel asked.

Anna smiled. "The more compelling the episode, the stronger marketing it becomes for the Bayview Inn. People love to visit businesses they've seen on television."

Joel nodded, obviously getting the message, so she moved on. There were a lot of basics to cover, including the promise that if they did their best to ignore the cameras at first, eventually they wouldn't have to work so hard at it. They didn't mind if homeowners looked at the cameras—it just added to the do-it-yourself feel they encouraged with cell phone video—but being too aware of them made people awkward and the conversations stilted.

They also had a short list of demolition-related jobs that were important to catch on camera—such as smashing tiles and pulling down horsehair plaster—and those would be scheduled with the crew so they could have multiple cameras filming.

"Also, if something fun happens, like finding old newspapers or a treasure in the walls, but the camera didn't catch it, we might do a little reenactment," she added. Then she decided it was time to stop talking and just begin the process. The only way for the family to get comfortable was to start doing it. "Today's all about being excited to pack up the last of the personal things and get started. We're going to go shoot the walk-and-talk while you get them ready, Eryn."

"Perfect. Tess, let's start with you."

"Start what with me?" Anna heard the older woman ask, but she didn't hear the answer because she was already heading for the front door with Mike on her heels.

He'd already gone through the run-through footage and determined the best camera angle, and with her nerves under control and Finn not watching her, Anna managed to get it done in one shot. Mike made her do it several more times, just to be sure, but she knew she'd already nailed it.

When she went back inside, she could hear footsteps upstairs, so she figured that was where the rest of the crew had decided to start the filming. But as she neared the kitchen, she heard a deep, inexplicably sexy voice that stopped her in her tracks.

She wouldn't mind hearing that voice whispering sweet nothings in her ear, that was for sure. But right now he didn't sound particularly happy. Or sweet.

"You are *not* putting makeup on my face."

Anna heard the frustration in Eryn's sigh, but she wasn't going to intercede yet. "We won't call it makeup, then. We'll call it…primer or something."

"Primer? Or spackling paste?"

The growl in Finn's voice made Anna want to giggle, so she pressed her lips together. Hearing her laugh at him wasn't going to improve his mood any.

"It's just a little powder," Eryn persisted. "So you're not too shiny if we have to use the lights for the indoor shots."

"It's going to be so hot today we could fry eggs on the sidewalk, but thanks to the humidity, they'll probably end up poached. So unless you're going to film me sitting on my ass in front of an air conditioner, I'm going to be shiny."

"Fine," she heard Eryn snap. "Go forth and be shiny, then."

When she heard chair legs scraping over the floor, Anna stepped into the kitchen. Eryn just rolled her eyes and closed the case of very basic makeup supplies they used. Luckily, being a show primarily featuring construction meant they didn't have to travel with a glam squad.

Then she looked at Finn, and when their eyes met, she could practically see his annoyance melting away. His lips quirked, not quite smiling, and she felt a flush of heat she hoped Eryn wouldn't notice.

"If I'm shiny later," he said, "blame me. Eryn tried."

"I heard." Anna shrugged. "We don't really do much, but we've found that even if people are tearing apart a house, they want to look good on television. Not that you have to worry about it."

A sound suspiciously like a choked-back snicker from Eryn's side of the table made Anna wince. She hadn't intended to imply it would take more than a little shine on TV to make Finn anything less than devastatingly handsome, but based on her assistant's reaction, she'd managed to do just that.

"Thank you," Finn said, his mouth curving into a grin. "I guess I'll go upstairs and see if they need me to lug boxes or whatever."

Because she knew she wouldn't be able to stop herself from watching him walk away, Anna nodded and then pulled her phone out of her back pocket to give herself something to look at besides his back. And his butt in those jeans.

She didn't look up until she heard his footsteps climbing the wooden staircase. After she was sure he was gone, she slid her phone back in her pocket and took a deep breath. She'd thought this project would be a challenge because of the secrets she had to keep—the real reason she'd taken it on, as well as Tess's fraudulent claims. But she definitely hadn't expected her desire for the handyman to be on that list.

"It's not supposed to be this hot in May, is it?" Eryn grimaced as she tugged her shirt away from her chest, fanning it a little as if it would send a breeze over her skin. "Or humid."

"You and I have both lived in Connecticut for over five years, so you know as well as I do that if it's hot in New England, it's humid."

"In May?" Her assistant shook her head, and then leaned closer to Anna. "It doesn't help that every time you and Finn are in the room together, the temperature spikes at least ten degrees."

It was Anna's turn to roll her eyes. "If you keep spouting that nonsense and somebody hears you, I'm going to make emptying the RV septic tanks your job from now on."

"Sure thing, boss." Eryn was still laughing when she picked up the case and walked out of the kitchen.

* * *

Finn could remember a time when he was young—maybe nine or ten—when he'd wanted more than anything to be a television star. He'd be the heroic lead of a science fiction series, maybe, like *Star Trek* or *Battlestar Galactica*. Or he'd star in Westerns, though he knew at some point he'd probably have to learn to ride a horse.

Right now, he'd never been so thankful to have outgrown a childhood whim. Even on as small a scale as he knew this production was, filming for a television show was proving to be something he didn't have the patience for.

Of course, it didn't help that his mother and grandmother kept bickering while his father heaved so many weary sighs that Finn was surprised he didn't pass out. After two hours spent listening to his grandmother spin her fictional yarn as they went through the guest rooms and her master bedroom upstairs, the crew had moved them downstairs. He got the impression they were slightly disappointed not to have more items of historical value to focus on.

If only they knew that *none* of the items had genuine historical value.

But them knowing the truth would be a disaster, so he kept his mouth shut and did what he was told, which was mostly moving boxes after the cameraman was done with a room.

When they cleared the living room and he was given the signal that everything in it could be moved to one of the storage pods, he sighed and got ready for more trips out into the brutal heat. The crew went into the kitchen, where he knew Anna was because he could hear her voice, but he ignored the urge to follow the others. The sooner he got stuff moved, the sooner he could go home, take a cold shower and catch up on the work he'd missed while playing handyman.

A frame he didn't recognize poking out of the box caught his eye and he stopped to set the box down so he could pull it out. Behind the glass was what appeared to be a very old newspaper article about the Bayview Inn and the struggles of the Weaver family to keep it going. The article carried a photo he did recognize, showing his grandparents on the front porch, with their three sons staggered in front of them, one to a step. Uncle Frank had died in a car accident when Finn was a baby, and Uncle Kent had married a woman who didn't like the rest of the family. The estrangement had gone on so long that Finn often forgot about him.

His mom turned the corner, holding a lamp so old it would probably be called retro if not for the fact it was so hideously ugly nobody would want it. He turned the frame to face her. "What is this?"

After peeking around the corner she'd just rounded to ensure nobody was nearby, she stepped close and kept her voice low. "Gram wrote that and got the newspaper to print it out on their paper. Then she dabbed tea all over it, crinkled it up, smoothed it out and left it in the sun to dry."

"You're kidding."

"That woman is an evil genius, Finn. Every night when I say my prayers, I thank the good Lord she doesn't have higher ambitions than getting a free renovation."

He laughed even though he wasn't sure she was joking. "This is the most ridiculous thing she's done yet, by far."

"Can't argue with that."

"This didn't just happen. I mean, there was prep work done and a lot of stuff already moved to those pods. Plus the permits. How come nobody told me until two days ago?"

"We didn't know, either. There were several advance visits, from what I gather. Two guys showed up to do an inspection and make sure the house has good bones and a solid foundation, since they do renovations, not structural rehab. And then the stuff you said. But she didn't bring us into the loop until *after* she'd signed the contract."

"How did she manage to hide that from us?" he asked. "Especially in this town. People moving stuff into storage pods at the Weaver house should have been the talk of Blackberry Bay."

"The moving part was very recent and she

claimed she had a very contagious head cold to keep your dad and me away, I guess, along with all of her nosy friends. As for the gossip, I assume it's all part of blackmailing people into going along with this ridiculousness."

Footsteps on the hardwood floor kept him from saying anything else, and he carried the box out to stack with the others in the pod. When he got back to the front porch, he found Anna there, holding out a bottle of water that was so cold it was already sweating in the heat.

"Thank you," he said, and then he held it against the back of his neck for a minute before cracking the cap off. He sat on the step and downed a quarter of the bottle in one shot. He was surprised when Anna sat on the wide step next to him. He didn't imagine he smelled too great right then. But with each of them sitting somewhat sideways, leaned against the railings, she wasn't *too* close. And he could see her face. "I needed this."

"Usually I'm better at making sure everybody remembers to hydrate, but my publicist decided today was the day he would dump a ton of questions about a book tour on Eryn and me."

"A book tour, huh?"

"Yeah, for my second book. Same themes as the show, of course, but not tie-ins so they're not connected to the network. I always like to keep my eggs in more than one basket."

"Always smart business," he said, before remembering he was supposed to know more about fixing a loose porch railing than business. "You're a little young to have built yourself an empire, aren't you?"

"And you're a little old to be mowing your grandmother's lawn, aren't you?"

"Ouch," he said, and the hand he put over his heart to signal being wounded was only a slight exaggeration. "I guess I deserved that."

She laughed and his heart thudded a little faster under his palm before he dropped his hand. "I wouldn't exactly call it an empire."

"And I do more than mow lawns." He wished he could tell her how much more.

"Touché." After she held eye contact for a long moment, her mouth almost curved into a smile, and she looked down at the ring she was spinning on her right hand. "To be perfectly honest, my primary marketable skill is being able to engage with a camera, and it was my YouTube channel that originally brought me to the network's attention. That's what enabled me to monetize my passion for fixing up really old houses."

"And where did that passion come from? For fixing up old houses, I mean. Did it start with a knack for design or from the actual houses?"

"The houses," she said without hesitation. "Nothing breaks my heart more than watching an old house with character deteriorate, knowing it's only a matter of time before it's replaced by a vinyl-clad box with windows. I've just always loved them. The details in the woodwork and old brick. Gingerbread trim and latticework and... don't even get me started. I could go on all day."

Her self-deprecating chuckle made him smile. "You light up when you talk about it, so feel free to go on as long as you want. Tell me how you ended up focusing on inns."

"Not just inns, which you'd know if you watched the show," she said, and then she laughed to show there were no hard feelings. "I've done a couple of restaurants, though they're a much bigger project because of the commercial kitchen aspect. I've done several houses where we turned the downstairs into office space, with the residence upstairs. A lot of people with big historical properties try to run businesses out of them to offset the cost, but it's really hard to make a modern business work efficiently in an antiquated setting. My focus on them is two-fold, I guess. One, those are the people who really care and are strongly motivated to preserve the property, and two, it's a hook. It gives viewers a stronger emotional investment in the show."

"And for every show you do, you probably manage to help a few more people who are in the same position. They get some tips or some ideas for resources, plus just the boost of knowing it can be done."

Her smile lit up her face and he had to take another gulp of chilled water to cool himself down. "Exactly. I just want to inspire people to see that not only are their houses worth saving, but that it can be done. Even if it's about three hundred degrees outside."

He chuckled as she wiped sweat from her forehead with the back of her hand. "I guess we're all shiny today. Tomorrow's supposed to be cooler, though. And less humid."

"That's a good thing, since we're starting demolition tomorrow."

"Can't wait," he muttered, unable to even pretend he was excited about the prospect.

"Hey, maybe we'll find some priceless treasure in the walls, like a copy of the Declaration of Independence or a signed Picasso," she said, her eyes crinkling with humor. "You never know. There could be something worth a lot of money in there."

"What's the going rate for petrified mouse carcasses these days?"

She pretended to give the matter serious thought for a few seconds. "Probably slightly less than mummified squirrel remains."

They were laughing softly together when the screen door opened and Eryn stepped onto the porch. "I *really* hate to interrupt, Anna, but Cody just asked Tess if the lemonade was made from concentrate and she's trying to throw him out."

Anna's eyes widened, which made Finn laugh as she stood and brushed off the seat of her capris. "Gram's pretty proud of her lemonade. She makes it fresh."

"So he insulted her." Anna sighed. "Any tips on smoothing it over?"

"It might be easier to hire a new cameraman," he said, because he'd agreed to fake being the family handyman, not the on-site therapist. Nobody paid him enough for that. But when Anna blew out a sharp breath, he couldn't help himself. "Maybe tell her the kid's never had lemonade that wasn't from a powdered mix and doesn't know any better. She might feel bad for him."

"She's a lot feistier than I expected," Anna said, shaking her head. "There's definitely a lot more to her than meets the eye."

"Oh, you have no idea," he muttered as the two women went inside to put out the first of what Finn suspected would be many fires.

Chapter Five

By Sunday, the entire crew was ready for a break. Even if they didn't film on-site, they often spent at least part of Sundays reviewing film or making a supply run. But a few days with the Weaver family had worn them all out, and Anna had told them all to take the day off. Eryn had driven off in the little car the previous morning and probably wouldn't be back until tomorrow night, so she had the RV to herself.

It was also Mother's Day, and Anna knew she wasn't going to be able to focus on her work. Rather than have to come up with an explanation for her distraction, she was going to enjoy some downtime in the RV with the AC cranked up and something mindless streaming on her iPad.

But first, she needed to call Naomi—the woman she'd called Mom for the first sixteen years of her life. And still did, because she was always going to be Mom to Anna.

Honey, you'll be moving out with me. Hailey and Casey are staying here. I... I'm sorry you have to find out this way, but Naomi isn't your birth mother. We got married when you were just a baby and it just seemed easier for her to be your mom. I always meant to tell you, but the time never seemed right.

Anna hadn't grasped what he meant right away, struggling to understand his emotional confession as they both cried. She'd been prepared for the divorce talk. Even a self-involved teenager could see that the cracks in their marriage had widened into chasms. She hadn't been prepared to learn her life was a lie, and that she'd only been told the truth because it would come out during the proceedings.

It had shaken her faith in her father—in marriage and in stability. Years later, her own marriage had crumbled in the same unexpected and devastating fashion, when a tabloid outed her husband's meetings with a show host from a rival network as being an affair, and not his real estate company trying to sell her house as he'd claimed. It was no wonder she'd given up on men and thrown herself into *Relic Rehab*.

Anna had gone with her father when he moved out. She didn't have to. Naomi had said she was welcome to stay with her and Anna's sisters, and at sixteen, the court would allow her to live with the woman who'd raised her. But in the end, she hadn't been able to face her father being all alone, even though she was so angry with him—even though he'd lied to her for her entire life. But her relationship hadn't ended with Naomi just because her father's marriage to her had.

This was the first Mother's Day Anna wasn't within driving distance of the traditional Mother's Day brunch. Getting together with her sisters and Naomi was easy when it was a group thing. But this was the first time since finding out her mom wasn't who she thought she was that Anna would have to deliberately reach out on her own.

The irony of her being in her birth mother's hometown for the occasion had Anna turning her phone over and over in her hand, hesitating. Being where she was and doing what she was doing had her emotions in a low-level but constant state of upheaval and she wasn't sure she was up to this phone call.

But she also wasn't up to disappointing Naomi. Their legal relationship may have been severed, but Naomi had worked so hard at making sure

Anna knew her love for her was genuine and that she wasn't going to stop loving her just because she wasn't married to Anna's dad anymore. Rather than letting her mind obsess over it all day—working herself into an emotional state that might show in her voice—Anna pulled up Naomi in her contacts and tapped her photo. It only rang one time.

"Anna! I was just thinking about you!"

The surprise and joy her mother—former stepmother—managed to inject into those few words made Anna smile, despite the pang of guilt she got from almost bailing on making the call. "Happy Mother's Day."

"Thank you, honey."

"I won't keep you long because I know you're getting ready for brunch, but I wanted you to know I'm thinking about you and wishing I could be there."

"I wish you could be with us, too." She sniffled, and Anna knew she was trying not to cry. "It won't be the same without you. Where are you filming?"

"I'm in… New Hampshire. An old inn on a lake. It's beautiful, actually." She'd almost admitted to being in Blackberry Bay because it was a bandage she'd have to rip off eventually, but at the last second she realized Mother's Day might not be the kindest day to tell the woman who'd raised her that she was looking for the woman who'd chosen not to. "I'll tell you all about it next time I see you."

"Let me know when you're going to be home and we'll have a ladies' lunch or something fun."

"Definitely," Anna said. They both kept their tones light, neither mentioning her father. They never did. And Anna didn't spend a lot of time in his home once she graduated because her father keeping secrets from her had seemed like a worse transgression than Naomi keeping secrets from her. While they were both at fault, Anna definitely heaped most of the blame on her dad's shoulders.

They made small talk for a few minutes, until there was a lull Anna could take advantage of. "I know you have to get ready for brunch and I have a lot of work to do, so I'll let you go."

"I'm so glad you called today."

"Me too." Anna hesitated, and then just went with her heart. "I love you, Mom."

"I love you too, honey. So much."

Once the call was over, Anna flopped down on her bed and stared at the ceiling. She was restless and needed something to occupy her time, but she knew her mind wasn't going to focus on anything for more than a few minutes. She probably could have talked Eryn into going for a walk with her, but before they'd even arrived in town, her assistant had scheduled this time off for herself. She and her wife had a little boy who was eleven months old and Eryn had wanted to be home for their first Mother's Day together.

Anna got tired of staring at the ceiling fairly quickly, so she got up and cleaned the RV, which took all of ten minutes. Then, still restless, she grabbed her phone and slid her slim wallet into her pocket. Maybe a walk would help.

It ended up being a longer walk than she intended. By the time she reached what passed for downtown Blackberry Bay, her hair was sticking to her neck and she regretted not thinking to put it in a ponytail. But there was a slight breeze off the water and she made her way to the gazebo where she and Eryn had shared a cupcake. She could sit here and look out over the lake. It was definitely a better view than the RV ceiling.

She wondered if her mother—her *birth* mother—had ever sat in this spot, looking out over the still water.

Anna knew almost nothing about her. A few times over the years, she'd plugged her name into a Facebook or Google search, but Christine Smith wasn't the easiest name to search. Anna's birth certificate said her mother had been born in New Hampshire, and her father had let slip during one of the few times she could get him to talk about her mother that he'd met her while on vacation in a town called Blackberry Bay, where Christine had been scooping ice cream for tourists. He'd been so reluctant to talk about her—only saying she hadn't been fit to be a mother—and it obviously pained him so much that she'd eventually stopped asking questions.

At any time since she turned sixteen, Anna probably could have done a deep dive and learned pretty much anything she might want to know about the woman who'd given birth to her. Especially in the last few years, when she had the financial resources to get a professional involved. But something had always held her back—more than the difficulty in narrowing down all the Christine Smiths in the state.

She hadn't wanted Anna. Christine Smith had walked away and let another woman claim her daughter as her own. So she might occasionally cave to curiosity and peek at a few search results, but mostly Anna had spent the last almost-ten years trying not to want her mother any more than she had wanted her.

Seeing the words *Blackberry Bay* on Tess Weaver's application had taken her breath away. Literally. She'd frozen, unable to breathe for a few seconds, with the paper trembling in her hand. In that moment, she'd realized she *did* care. She wanted to at least know who the woman was, and this was clearly a sign that it was time. The opportunity presented itself and she took it, even though it meant juggling a lot of secrets.

The deep rumble of a Harley-Davidson engine broke into her thoughts and she turned in time to see a black motorcycle cruise past at a low speed. Even though the rider was wearing a helmet, she recognized Finn, and since he didn't see her, she allowed herself to drink in the sight of him as he made his way down the main street.

Once he was out of sight, she sighed and hit the screen to wake up her phone. Even though she felt ridiculous doing it, she opened her Facebook app and punched his name into the search box. There were definitely fewer Finn Weavers than Christine Smiths and it didn't take her long to find him. Unfortunately, he appeared to be one of those people who not only grasped privacy settings but made use of them, and she couldn't see anything but his name and profile picture, but the Harley in the photo looked like his.

After clearing her search history, she put the phone back to sleep and resumed staring at the water. Another mystery, she thought. Who was Finn Weaver when he wasn't pretending to be his grandmother's handyman?

He had money, she thought. That motorcycle wasn't cheap. And she recognized the brand of his boots and his jeans. Maybe not enough money to throw around—or remodel the Bayview Inn—but he did okay for himself.

What did he really do for a living? Where did he live? And, most important, was there a significant other in his life?

So many questions, she thought. She only hoped she could get answers to some of them soon, so the risks she was taking—maybe even the loss of her job, her crew's jobs and her professional reputation—by being here under Tess's false pretenses were worth it.

Finn quite literally breathed a sigh of relief when he passed the Thank You for Visiting Blackberry Bay sign on his way out of town on Sunday afternoon.

He needed a break. A break from the wacky pretend world his grandmother had them all living in. A break from the bickering sparked by Gram and his mom temporarily living under the same roof. And a break from the constant struggle to ignore the raging desire he felt for Anna Beckett every time he laid eyes on her.

Hell, he didn't even have to see her. All he had to do was hear her name—or think it—and his body was all *yup, she's the one*. Between the effort it took to hide his reactions to her, the work hours he was putting in on the computer after a long day pretending to be a handyman, and the sleep he was losing while imagining all the different ways he'd like to touch and *be* touched by Anna, he was mentally and physically exhausted.

A night in his own apartment would do wonders for him. He hoped. At the very least, if he lay awake thinking about Anna, he'd be doing it on his very firm king-size mattress and not in the old double bed of his youth. Or, thanks to Gram, his present. Sleeping on it once in a while during visits to his parents was one thing. Sleeping on it every night after a day of labor at his grandmother's fake inn was entirely another, especially with the amount of Anna-induced tossing and turning he was doing.

The ride did a lot to clear his head, though. It always did, especially when he got close to Portsmouth and had to really pay attention in the traffic. By the time he parked his bike and grabbed what he needed out of the saddlebags, he felt almost himself again.

He closed the door of his apartment and then leaned against it with a relieved sigh. Silence. He rarely appreciated his quiet neighborhood more than he did the first few minutes he was home after a visit to his family.

Finn's phone rang, startling him out of his melancholy, and he sighed when he saw the number for his parents' landline on his screen. They each used their cell phones to call him, which meant it was probably Gram.

"Where are you?" she demanded as soon as he answered.

"I told you I have meetings tomorrow that I

can't miss. Tom lined everything up so we can do it in one day, but I do have a business to run, Gram."

"You didn't tell Anna or anybody from the crew you were going, did you?"

He chuckled. "Did I tell Anna that your handyman had to leave for Portsmouth because he's meeting some very rich executives from Boston for lunch? No, I didn't."

"I'll have to come up with some reason why you're not there for when she asks me where you are."

"I doubt she's going to care. She probably won't even realize I'm gone."

Gram's laugh made him pull the phone away from his ear for a second. "I've seen the way you two look at each other. She'll wonder where you are."

Her words both horrified and thrilled him. It was nice to know he wasn't alone in feeling the chemistry between him and Anna. But on the flip side, knowing she might be as interested in exploring that chemistry as he was just made it suck all the more that he couldn't act on it.

"You're imagining things, Gram," he said firmly, even though she probably wasn't. The last thing he needed was for her to get it into her head to play matchmaker and *really* mess everything up. "I'll be there Tuesday morning, ready to play handyman."

"You're a good boy, Finn."

Her voice was thick with not only affection, but a little bit of apology, and it made him smile. "I love you, Gram."

"I love you, too. Your mom just started yelling about something, so I should probably go."

"Yelling about *something*?"

"I was nice and rearranged all her kitchen drawers for her. Honestly, I don't know how she could find anything the way they were."

"Gram."

"Oh, she's coming closer. I'll see you Tuesday." She hung up on his laughter, and he shook his head as he plugged the phone in to charge. It was too bad he was commuting on the Harley, or he could have invited his dad along with him. He had a comfortable couch, not that it would matter to Joel at this point. He'd probably happily sleep on Finn's floor just to get away from the two women in his life at the moment.

The next morning, Finn managed to get to the office before Tom, so he was able to brew the coffee and put out the fresh doughnuts he'd picked up on the way. Even though he knew his business partner was okay with him being out of the office for a while, Finn felt as if he needed to make it up to him somehow.

"I smell coffee and doughnuts," Tom said as soon as he walked through the door. "Please don't tell me you feel guilty because you're about to tell me you're going into some kind of witness protection program to hide from your family and you can't be my partner anymore."

"As appealing as that sounds right now, no. I'm not sure even the US Marshals Service could keep me hidden from Mom and Gram. And I'd have to leave Grizz, too. That would suck." When Tom paused to arch an eyebrow at him over the rim of his coffee mug, Finn chuckled. "Also, I would never do that to you, of course."

"Dare I ask how things are going with Tess?"

Finn slowly shook his head, blowing out a long breath. "I don't even know how to explain what's happening there. Or in her head. It's a little unreal, actually."

"I think what's unreal is anybody thinking you'd be even a halfway decent handyman."

Finn laughed. "I guess the fact I'm *not* is part of the story, since a halfway decent handyman probably would have kept the house in better shape. Excuse me, the *inn*."

He'd called Tom the first night in Blackberry Bay and filled him in on what was going on. He told him everything, not only because he needed his business partner to be okay with holding down the office alone, but because if there was even a hint of liability on Finn's part with regard to deceiving the production company, it could be an issue. But Tom had only laughed. He'd laughed so long, actually, that Finn had told him about everything *except* Gram's baby oil suggestion. Tom was a good enough friend to ensure that Finn would never live that down.

Tom's phone chimed and he glanced at it. "We've got to leave now if we want to be there to greet the clients at the restaurant. And remind me to confirm their golf reservations on the way. It was easier for me to set it up for them, since I play there with my father-in-law."

"Hey, I just want to tell you how much I appreciate you being cool with this."

Tom shrugged. "You know as well as I do that most of our work is done on the computer, so you can do it anywhere. And you are. The meetings we can handle. It's not like you have to schedule flights or anything."

"Still, I appreciate it."

"It's no problem. Now let's get these meetings out of the way so you can get back to being handy."

Finn grabbed a balled-up piece of paper out of the trash to throw at him, but Tom dodged it and just laughed harder.

"Maybe we should add it to your business cards," Tom said as he pulled open the door, and they were still laughing when they got into the car.

As the day went on, though, Finn found himself wishing he was in Blackberry Bay. The homesickness always set in, despite the fact he *technically* was home. Even though they were a *lot* at times, he loved his parents and Gram fiercely and being only an hour away felt like too far most of the time.

It was what they'd wanted for him, though. He was a smart kid with big dreams. He had a good work ethic and everybody rooted for him. Especially his teachers. There was no limit to what he'd be able to do if he put his mind to it.

That was Finn in high school. Most likely to succeed. Mostly likely to get the hell out of Blackberry Bay. Most likely to make his parents proud by going off into the world and making a bunch of money so he didn't have to work as hard as they did.

But Finn now? He'd tried. He got his degree and thought about the big money to be made in New York City, but the city held no appeal for him. He'd settled in Boston for a while. Hated it. Then he met Tom, who also hated Boston, and together they landed in Portsmouth. A small city not only close enough to Boston to do business there, but a city that maintained a historical, almost small-town feel that appealed to both men. And it was only an hour from his hometown.

He was thankful for that. And business was good, his family was healthy, and he'd managed to rent one of the few apartments in his neighborhood that had a small garage to park his bike out of the rain. Life was good, if a little lonely at times.

But his heart was always in Blackberry Bay, and there were times he wanted to pack it up and go home, and to hell with everybody's expectations.

Chapter Six

Four days later, Finn thought he must've been out of his mind to miss Blackberry Bay. He was *this* close to packing up his stuff, resigning his position of fake handyman, and heading out of town. And if he did, he wasn't coming back until this *Relic Rehab* nonsense was done with.

His family was going to be the death of him. They were all spending *way* too much time with each other, and the old joke about nothing ruining a marriage faster than a husband and wife remodeling a house together wasn't all that funny anymore.

Now it was two o'clock in the afternoon, he was

exhausted and he'd gone straight past shiny and right to downright slimy before he got coated in plaster dust. It felt as if he'd been covered in batter and was slowly roasting in the hot oven that was the upstairs hall.

Just in case that wasn't fun enough, he'd heard Mike tell Cody to stay on Finn and Tess while he covered Joel and Alice, and the younger guy was going all in on his assignment. Finn was doing his best to ignore the camera, as Anna had told them to do, but it was like having somebody staring at him intently. Constantly. Without blinking.

He heard footsteps coming up the stairs and he knew it would be Anna because that was how his luck ran these days.

"Good news," she said once she'd reached the top and Cody had adjusted to get her and Tess in the shot together. "Eryn just spoke to your electrician and he can come over as soon as he wraps up his current job. Probably an hour at the most."

Finn wasn't thrilled about one of his best friends being sucked into his grandmother's scheme, but it didn't surprise him Gram had given them his name when they were lining up contractors. The way he understood it, when *Relic Rehab* did projects in places they worked a lot—along the coastline or in the greater Boston area—they had contractors they used all the time, probably for a discounted rate. But Blackberry Bay was far enough away so it was cheaper for them to hire local. Plus it fit into the whole do-it-almost-yourself vibe of the show.

There were a couple of benefits for Finn, too. The first being that Brady Nash loved Gram almost like his own, so he'd be careful about what he said. But, more important, it would be nice to have somebody around who not only knew the entire truth of the situation Finn had been dragged into, but somebody he could confide in. Somebody who could help remind him of the many good reasons he had for not acting on the sexual tension simmering between him and Anna.

As a rivulet of sweat tracked through the plaster dust treacherously close to his eye, Finn muttered a few choice curse words under his breath and yanked his T-shirt up so he could use the hem to mop the worst of it from his forehead and face. With the way the four Weavers were going home at the end of each day, *Relic Rehab* was going to have to add a new washer and dryer for his mother to their budget.

After he dropped the T-shirt back into place, Finn's gaze just happened to land on Anna's face. They didn't lock eyes, though, because hers were zeroed on his stomach. Specifically, the abs he'd just covered with the filthy shirt.

Then she blinked and he noticed she looked everywhere but at his face, and she cleared her throat before speaking again. "There's not much we can do up here until the electrician arrives and I don't see any point in starting something else in the amount of time we have, so let's take a break. Get a snack. And hydrate. Drink a *lot* of water."

Then she spun around and went back downstairs so fast he was afraid for a few seconds she'd fall. She didn't, though, and Finn leaned against one of the exposed wall studs with a heavy sigh.

He'd known this renovation would be more extensive than their usual projects—Anna had explained to them it would be their big makeover of the season, plus there was the horsehair lath and plaster to deal with—but seeing his grandmother's house torn apart like this still made him uneasy. It was as though they'd reached a point of no return and no matter what happened—or how much he wanted to sneak off with Anna and kiss her until he got that out of his system—they all had to see this through.

Even though they'd actually reached the point of no return when his grandmother signed her name on the bottom line, the deception seemed to weigh more heavily on him every day, and he'd be glad when it was all over and he could go back to his life.

Unfortunately, he relaxed against the stripped wall too long and Cody was able to gather his equipment and get to the stairs before Finn made his escape. And, as he'd feared, as soon as they were alone, Gram gave him a smug look.

"I told you," she said, hands on her hips. "You two spend more time watching each other than the camera does watching us."

"*That* is an exaggeration and you know it," he said, deliberately keeping his voice barely above a whisper in hopes she would, too.

"Not by much."

"Gram, please don't do this." He shoved a hand through his hair, wincing when he hit a chunk of plaster. "This is hard enough without you making things awkward. *More* awkward, actually."

She sighed. "Fine. I'm not wrong, but I don't want to make things harder for you."

"I would hug you, but I'm pretty disgusting right now." His grandmother, playing the part of frail elderly lady, was far less filthy than the rest of them, of course. But she wrapped her arms around his waist and hugged him anyway, so he squeezed her back. "I'd go spray myself with the garden hose, but I'm afraid this mess would harden into some kind of full-body cast."

"Let's go get a drink," Gram said. "Supervising you lot is thirsty work."

A short time later, Finn was sitting blessedly alone on the porch steps and staring down into his almost empty plastic cup of lemonade when he heard the sound of a cell phone camera shutter.

He lifted his head and saw Brady standing in the driveway. His friend laughed at him for a few seconds before doing who-knew-what with the picture he'd just taken.

"Who are you sending that to?"

"Reyna." Brady finished tapping at his screen and then slid the phone into his pocket. "And to you. If Tom gives you a hard time about being away, you can send him that so he knows you're not really downing umbrella drinks on a tropical beach somewhere."

"The last place I want to be is someplace even more hot and humid than here. I probably wouldn't turn down a drink right now, though, even if it comes with an umbrella."

"As wrung out as you look right now, it would only take one drink and you'd be singing bad karaoke duets with whoever got too close to you."

Finn knocked back the last gulp of lemonade and pushed himself to his feet, trying not to groan and give Brady more ammunition. "They were holding off on starting the next thing on their endless list until you got here, so they're probably ready for us."

Brady went in first, and Finn was expecting the surprised noise his friend made. Between the family and the *Relic Rehab* crew—which included two laborers named Frankie and Jim, along with Mike and Cody, who filled in as needed when not filming—

they'd gotten a lot down and the house was almost entirely studs at this point. They wanted Brady to run point on some electrical work and then they'd start hanging Sheetrock.

Then Brady stopped so short Finn almost walked into him. "What the hell?"

"Who is that?"

Finn followed his gaze through the open walls and saw Anna standing in front of the kitchen window with her hands on her hips. It looked as if she was talking to herself, but he saw the little white earphone and realized she was probably on a call. Then he looked back at his friend and was surprised to see the back of Brady's neck had a pink flush.

That wasn't okay. Not by a long shot. Not only was Brady off the market, but Finn had dibs. Nobody knew that but him, of course, but still. He didn't want another guy, even—or maybe especially—his best friend having any kind of chemistry with her.

"She's the star of the show. Anna Beckett." When Brady didn't respond or even move, Finn nudged him with his elbow. "Earth to Brady, the guy with the hot new wife and the cutest baby boy in town."

He could get away with saying that because his own nephews didn't actually live *in* Blackberry Bay.

"She look familiar to you at all?" Brady muttered, still not taking his eyes off of Anna.

"She's on TV. She probably looks familiar to a lot of people."

"I guess." Brady seemed to shake off whatever had made him freeze up, and he shrugged. "That makes sense, though I'd swear I've met her before. You know anything about her?"

"Not as much as I'd like to," he said easily, but it was enough to catch Brady's attention. He didn't need to call dibs because Brady was married to Reyna, whom he'd been in love with since first grade. And luckily, it seemed as if Brady had been struck by déjà vu and not attraction.

"It's like that, huh?"

Finn shrugged. "It's complicated."

"That's a given, with Tess involved. What a freakin' mess this is." He snorted and shook his head. "Bayview Inn."

"I've been meaning to ask you about that, actually." The question had popped into his head a few times, but never when he could call Brady. "Why didn't you call and tell me this was happening? Maybe I could have stopped her."

Brady held up his hands. "First, by the time I was involved, the papers were probably already signed. And the woman who called me about doing the job was rushed and she just gave me the address and asked my rate for old work—for doing remodel wiring—but she never mentioned this house being an inn. I recognized the address of course, but I was mostly just happy Tess had found a way to get some help with the place. I didn't know about the inn part."

Finn knew he was right about the ink probably already being dry on the contracts, but it still got on his nerves that in a town where everybody seemed to know—and tell—everything, his grandmother had managed to sneak this one right past her family.

"It's still hard to believe she was able to get all the way through the preliminary process without my parents or me knowing about it. The one bit of gossip that actually mattered."

Brady nodded. "She's a smart lady. And speaking of ladies, let's go back to gossiping about the complicated situation between you and Anna. What's stopping you?"

"There's the fact my family is conning her production company out of who even knows how much money."

"But are they really? The production company's getting their episodes out of it and I've known your family my whole life. They'll be entertaining episodes, for sure."

"Brady!" Gram called, and Finn had to fight not to roll his eyes when she took a couple of steps toward them before remembering to slow her pace and hunch over a little.

"What is Tess wearing?" Brady murmured to him. "And did she hurt herself? Why is she walking like that?"

"Don't ask," Finn said wearily. "Just go along with…everything."

"Measure twice. Cut once."

Alice gave her husband a look that could have sliced through the Sheetrock they were arguing about, as if it was butter. "Spare me the construction platitudes handed down from your father… the car salesman."

Anna was doing her best to be invisible as the husband and wife did their thing. Couples like the Weavers were her favorite to work with, and it wasn't the bickering alone. That made for good television, as long as it wasn't *mean* bickering. Marital banter shored up by decades of affection, though—the viewers ate that up. And so did Anna.

"When he wasn't selling cars, my dad did a lot of projects at home. How do you think I learned how to do things around the house?"

"Too bad he didn't teach you how to finish them," Alice said, and Anna tensed a little, but Joel just laughed.

"If I finish my projects, you'll have no reason to keep me around." Then he hooked his arm around his wife's face and pulled her close enough to plant a kiss on her temple.

Besides enjoying Joel and Alice's dynamic on a personal level—relationship goals, she thought—it was always a relief when the property owners and their friends and family filmed well. Especially on this project, but recognizing they were going to have a couple of great episodes of *Relic Rehab* went a long way toward easing the anxiety and guilt that selecting the Bayview Inn had saddled her with.

"We're losing the light," Mike said, breaking into her thoughts. "It makes more sense to wrap for the day and let Frankie and Jim get in here."

He was right, so she nodded. They had plenty of footage of the Weaver family hanging Sheetrock. It was time to let the guys go in and knock out the rest. They wouldn't get everything done before filming started again tomorrow, of course, but the Weavers could move on to the taping and mudding in the rooms they did finish.

Usually, to keep a project from falling behind, Anna would have the guys go in and do the more time-consuming work off camera, though she really preferred to stick to the DIY theme as closely as possible. She didn't think having Frankie and Jim around was cheating, since most people had at least a couple of people in their lives who could help them out. And filming a purely do-it-yourself renovation in real time would kill the show, so she had the two laborers, and there was fine print in the credits acknowledging their part in the renovation. They'd be lucky if they could finish two episodes in a year, otherwise.

"I think the others were doing the big paint color debate in the living room if you want to let them know," Mike said.

"We are *not* letting your mother choose the colors without us," Alice told her husband. "Hurry up and finish this."

"I need a drink first," Joel said. "And Finn's probably with her, so she can't go too rogue."

"I'll check on them," Anna said, since there was nothing left for her to do in this room.

It wasn't a long walk to the living room, but it gave Anna's brain enough time to relax. And when her mind was left to its own devices, images of Finn immediately popped in to occupy her thoughts.

It had been hard enough to concentrate on something besides Finn before. But now she had a new image—him lifting his T-shirt to reveal a taut stomach she immediately wanted to run her hands over—and she knew her imagination was going to have fun with that one.

He'd seen her looking, too. She hadn't been able to tear her gaze away before he dropped the hem of his shirt and looked up. It was going to take all of her self-control not to blush when she saw him again.

"You can't paint the walls salmon pink, Gram."

She heard him before she saw him, and the exasperation mingled with affection and humor in his voice made her smile.

"I can do whatever I want," Tess replied.

Not wanting to interrupt and kill the flow of the scene, Anna leaned against the doorjamb to watch Finn run a hand through his hair. Tess must have been particularly stubborn over the last several hours, because his hair was standing up in all directions and his fingers had worked nearly all of the plaster dust out.

"First of all, Gram, the clapboards are salmon pink. Your exterior and your interior walls can't be the same color. That would be weird."

"I prefer eccentric."

"And I feel like it would make all those *guests* you're going to have feel sick to their stomachs."

When Tess's eyes narrowed, Anna had to press her lips together to keep from chuckling, even as her stomach tightened with anxiety. Finn's emphasis on the word *guests* had her wondering if he could be pushed far enough to blow up the entire scheme just to get out of it.

She didn't think he would. He knew the stakes for Tess and it was obvious he would do whatever he had to in order to get her out of this. But any man could only take so much.

"The salmon pink on the outside doesn't make them sick," Tess shot back.

"Because it's outside, where it belongs. It would be too much in here, and it would probably do weird things to the lighting." Then, even though she hadn't moved, Anna must have popped up in Finn's peripheral vision because he turned his head slightly and smiled at her.

Anna was aware of Cody picking up his head and seeing her standing there. She saw the flash of his hand that signaled to Tess he'd stopped recording. But she was too busy looking into Finn's eyes to care.

She was in so much trouble.

Whatever this pull was, he felt it, too. And it was so strong that she seriously doubted her ability to hide it for the duration of this renovation.

"We're wrapping it up for the day," she said when she realized they were *all* looking at her and not just Finn. "It's a little early, but we want to give the guys a head start on hanging the rest of the Sheetrock, and I've got some work I need to do back at the RV."

"We should go right now," Tess said to her grandson. "If we beat your parents back to the house, we'll have plenty of hot water."

"A good son would say scheming to use up my

parents' hot water before they get home is wrong," he said. "But I think I'm going to need an entire hour in the shower. Let's go."

Because an image of Finn naked in the shower was just what Anna needed today. "Maybe a pre-shower with a garden hose?"

"I could use a cold shower right about now."

The way he said it—and the way his eyes crinkled with amusement—let her know he was saying exactly what she thought he was. And she was definitely going to need a cold shower of her own.

He took a step toward her and she knew without a doubt that if they were alone, he would take more steps, until he closed the distance between them. She could practically feel his arm sliding around her waist. His other hand cupping the back of her neck. His mouth claiming hers.

"Finn, let's go." Tess wasn't kidding about beating Joel and Alice home, and when she tugged at Finn's arm, he gave Anna one last sizzling look that promised all sorts of things if he could get her alone.

Definitely a cold shower, she thought as they walked out the door. Maybe two. One with the RV's outside shower and then another inside.

Several hours and one cool shower later, Anna closed her notebook and rubbed the back of her neck. The RV was definitely nice, but it wasn't the most ergonomically friendly of workplaces. She'd eaten a turkey sandwich and salad at the dinette, working on her voiceover scripts for previously shot footage, and she could only do that for so long before she needed a break.

She knew Eryn was in the other, larger RV with the crew, reviewing what they'd shot that day, so she grabbed a bottle of water from the fridge and went in search of company. As she neared the crew's motor home, she could hear them laughing and assumed they were watching a funny scene with Joel and Alice, or maybe Tess being Tess.

Until she opened the door and they not only stopped laughing, but looked guilty about being caught. There was throat clearing and a noticeable lack of eye contact.

She closed the door behind her to keep the air conditioning in and decided to focus her attention on Cody, who was the weakest link when it came to hiding things from her. "How's the footage from today?"

"We got some great stuff," Cody said. "What's the MPAA rating for *Relic Rehab* again?"

Anna frowned when they all made ridiculous noises in an effort to cover their snickers. "What are you talking about?"

Mike gave Cody a look that should have set the younger cameraman on fire on the spot, but only made him squirm. "Nothing, *boss*."

If he was having to remind Cody and the others of who she was with such emphasis, something was definitely up. "Spill it."

"We should go over the sheet for tomorrow," Eryn said, and Anna appreciated the effort, but it wasn't going to work.

"Cody," she said in a very I'm-the-boss tone. "Let's see it."

Mike sighed and waved a hand toward the screen. He was trying to look exasperated, but she'd known him too long to miss the amusement lurking in the lines of his face. They'd definitely been having a laugh at her expense before she stepped into the RV.

Cody queued up the footage and Anna folded her arms across her chest as she identified the upstairs hallway. It had been tight for filming, so it had been just Finn working while Tess pretended she was helping him. The scenes between those two always made her smile because Finn's love for his grandmother always came through loud and clear.

Cody scrubbed through the video until Anna's face appeared on the screen, and she felt heat spread over her skin all over again. Hopefully the dim light in the RV would hide it from the rest of the team, but watching Finn lift his shirt—exposing that taut stomach—to wipe his face had jacked up her temperature the first time, and the view was no less potent the second time. Then Cody repeated the clip, but this time he used the controls to zoom in on Anna's face.

The on-screen version of herself looked as though she was on day three of a no-carb diet and somebody had just set a bowl of baked macaroni and cheese in front of her.

Oh no. But yes, she actually looked as if she desperately wanted to devour the dish in front of her. Unfortunately, the dish was Finn. And just in case the visual wasn't enough, the microphone clearly picked up her needy sigh of desire that sounded as though it had sprung up from the very depths of her soul.

And all three of them were staring at her—watching her watch herself very obviously mooning over Finn Weaver's naked torso like a teenager.

"I mean, look at those abs," she finally said, trying to play it off as a totally normal reaction to the sight of smoothly muscled skin. "And you can delete that footage."

"Sure thing," Cody said, but he picked up his soda can and took a long sip.

"Oh no, I'm going to stand here and watch you do it," Anna added in a firm voice. "Delete it."

As he went through the process of eradicating the evidence, she was a little sorry she didn't have her own copy. Or at least a still picture. But when

Cody gave her the thumbs-up to indicate it was gone, she knew it didn't matter.

It was going to be a long time before she forgot that view.

Chapter Seven

On Monday morning, Anna sent Eryn with the crew in the SUV to the Bayview Inn. She had a few phone calls to make—including one with the network suits—and rather than having her assistant hovering over her and checking her watch every thirty seconds, she told them she'd catch up when she was done.

When that business was done, she found herself reluctant to drive straight to the Weaver house, though. She'd already been in Blackberry Bay for a couple of weeks and she hadn't yet started looking for information about her birth mother. The risk she'd taken when she'd accepted Tess's application would be for nothing if she left knowing nothing more about her mother than she had when she'd arrived.

She needed to make a list and then start checking things off. The records at town hall. Maybe the school kept old copies of yearbooks. Property records. But she needed to come up with a way of framing requests that didn't tip people off to the reason she was digging.

On a whim, she parked the car in the municipal lot. After making sure the small notebook she used for personal notes was in her bag, she started walking toward a small café she'd seen on Cedar Street one time she and Eryn were driving through town.

She could have a nice breakfast while coming up with a solid plan. At the very least she would be doing *something*.

A woman about Alice Weaver's age was walking toward her and glanced up from her phone as they got close. Then she frowned—a brief hesitation in her step—before she shook her head slightly and went back to her phone screen.

It wasn't the first time it had happened, but this time a new thought crept into her head. That reaction—the moment of confusion and then shaking it off—came from people that were all of a similar age group. An age group that would probably include Christine Smith. The people of Blackberry

Bay weren't feeling that sense of vague recognition because Anna was on TV.

She looked like her mother.

Throughout her childhood, she'd realized she didn't look a lot like either of her parents, but genetics were weird and fickle. She always assumed—maybe with a little nudging from her parents—that she looked like a grandparent, even though she didn't remember ever seeing photos of her dad's parents, who had passed away.

When she caught a funny look from another passing pedestrian, Anna realized she'd stopped walking and was simply standing in the middle of the sidewalk.

She looked enough like Christine Smith to make people who'd known her do double takes. Her mother had to have lived in this town until at least close to adulthood for the citizens to have known her well enough to see the resemblance a twenty-seven-year-old stranger held to her.

Do you know Christine Smith?

It would be such an easy question to ask. It was the most common surname in the country, as she'd discovered the few times she'd succumbed to the temptation to search for her birth mother's name.

When she reached the Cedar Street Café, she stepped inside and looked around for a good place to sit. It would probably make sense to take a seat at the counter, but if somebody sat next to her, she'd lose the privacy she wanted for making her list.

Then a diner sitting alone at a booth by the window lifted his head and Anna found herself staring directly into Finn Weaver's eyes.

Her breath caught and the split second when she might have been able to look away and pretend she hadn't seen him passed. When he smiled and gestured to the spot across from him, she told herself to mouth the words *thanks, but no* and take a seat at the counter. But what she did was return his smile and start walking toward his table.

He closed the laptop that had been sitting open in front of him and then capped the pen that was on a notebook next to the computer. By the time she reached him, he was stowing the work away, but as she sat down, Anna noticed a couple of things.

That was a very expensive laptop he was sliding into a leather case. Even more interestingly, the man used a *very* nice, heavy-looking enamel pen. She still wasn't sure exactly what Finn did when he wasn't pretending to do odd jobs around his grandmother's house, but she was willing to bet he wore a suit and tie.

She'd really like to see that.

"Fancy meeting you here," he said, setting the laptop case on the bench beside him before clipping the pen onto the notebook cover and setting them on top.

"Since I'm running late today anyway, I thought I'd have some breakfast on the way." She'd have to save her list for later, since she certainly couldn't make notes about her mother in front of Finn.

She wanted to ask about the laptop—it felt weird to ignore its presence—but she didn't want to go poking at his secrets. That would only invite him to start poking at hers, and it was in everybody's best interests for her to keep her motives for being in Blackberry Bay to herself.

"I just finished, but I'm always up for more coffee if you don't mind company while you eat."

"If I didn't want company, I would have sat at the counter. It would be rude to sit at your table and then throw you out."

He chuckled, and then looked up as the server approached. "Hey, Rissa. Have you met Anna yet?"

"I haven't. First time here?"

"Yes. I'm in town with *Relic Rehab*, doing the renovation on the Bayview Inn."

"Right." The corners of Rissa's mouth twitched, but Anna had to admire the way she kept her composure. It was a testament to Tess's standing in the community that everybody in Blackberry Bay was just going along with her story. "What can I get for you this morning?"

Since she'd had a doughnut already, she decided a little protein would be nice, so she ordered scrambled eggs with cheddar and a side of bacon. With coffee, of course.

"So be honest with me," Finn said when they were alone again, and Anna's stomach tightened. "On a scale of amusing to making you question your career choice, how is my family to work with?"

Relief made her short laugh sound a little breathier than she intended. "I think your family's great. We all do, actually. We're having a lot of fun on this project."

Skepticism made his eyebrow arch in an adorable way. "Fun?"

"Yes, fun. Renovating is stressful for people and you'd be surprised how often the bickering goes from lighthearted and affectionate, like your family's, to being really unpleasant to watch. That's why some episodes have more of *me* in them. The more Anna you see, the less usable footage of the property owners there was."

"I don't think more of you could be a bad thing." He shifted as he spoke, and his calf brushed hers. Neither of them pulled away.

Conscious of the warmth of his leg against hers, she smiled. "They might not even have room for me in the Bayview Inn's episodes. I'll probably do more voiceover work than actual filming."

"Feel free to leave me on the cutting room floor," he replied, obviously only half-jokingly.

Heat flooded her cheeks as she thought of the footage she'd made Cody delete last night, and she lifted her coffee cup to her mouth in an effort to hide it from him. Judging by the sparkle in his eyes, it didn't work.

"You and Tess together are my favorite part, though your parents together run a very close second," she said, trying to stay on topic. "As we start doing some of the more fun stuff like painting and fixtures—and by fun, I mean sometimes it's more fun for the viewer than the homeowner—we'll probably mix you together more. And you know when it comes to putting the kitchen back together, I'm going to pair up Alice and Tess."

He groaned and shook his head. "Remind me to call in sick for those days. And you make sure you have your hard hat on."

"It must be fun living with them both right now." She tilted her head, deciding to poke just a little. "Because I got the impression you're all staying in your parents' house together. Do you live with them all the time?"

When he got very still for a few seconds, she knew she'd pushed a button she shouldn't have. But while it was important not to blow up any lies Tess was telling, Anna wanted to know more about Finn. More *true* things.

"I have my own place," he said. "It's…outside

of town. I guess it's easier just to stay with them while we're working on Gram's house—the inn."

Anna recognized the way he answered the question without offering any actual information. She'd already guessed he lived outside of Blackberry Bay because he struck her as the kind of guy who would have seen to some of the repairs his grandmother's house needed if he was around. The question was *how far* outside of town he lived.

Rissa brought her breakfast, and the interruption gave Anna a chance to check the time. She winced, realizing Eryn was probably already wondering where she was, and she hadn't even eaten yet. Explaining that she was hanging out in a café with Finn wasn't something Anna wanted to do.

It was hard to eat with his leg pressed against hers, but she couldn't bring herself to move her foot. Maybe it wasn't as much contact as she'd like to have, but it was enough to keep her body practically humming with anticipation. Her body was doomed to disappointment, of course, but she decided to enjoy it while it lasted.

"Since the Bayview Inn has been passed down generationally, I assume you and your parents have always lived in Blackberry Bay?" she asked in between bites.

"Born and raised."

"So you know everybody in town, then?" She

was on thin ice, and she knew she had to tread carefully.

"Most people, I guess. There are always people moving away and new people moving in, of course."

She nodded, trying to think of a way she could ask about any Smith families without being too obvious, but she couldn't. There was no way to casually ask if he knew of a woman named Christine Smith.

When he asked her how she liked the RV life, the moment was gone, so she relaxed and ate her breakfast while they talked about life filming *Relic Rehab*. He was easy to talk to, and even though she knew he was probably trying to keep *her* from asking too many questions, he seemed genuinely interested in her answers.

When Rissa dropped off the bill, Anna noticed she'd combined their meals and reached for the paper, but Finn was faster. "I invited you to join me."

"But I have an expense account," she countered.

Maybe it was just wishful thinking on her part, but it felt as though his leg pressed a little more firmly against hers. "But it wasn't really a business breakfast, was it?"

"No," she said, because if she was being honest with herself, the last thing she wanted to do with Finn was talk about the show.

The first thing she wanted to do with him was… not allowed.

"Thank you for breakfast, then." She surrendered graciously, and managed to stifle her sigh of disappointment when he moved his leg and broke off the contact between them. Her watch buzzed and she looked at the notification. "And there's Eryn, wondering if I got lost."

"You can go if you need to. I'll settle up with Rissa and I have a couple of things I want to finish up before I join you all in Gram's fun house."

Laughing, Anna slid out of the booth and picked up her bag. "Don't be too long or there's no telling what colors Tess will pick for the walls."

"Last night she told Mom she should let her paint the guest room salmon pink so she can see if it does weird things to the lighting. I'm pretty sure Mom called the hardware store and told them to ban Gram unless she's accompanied by a member of the family." Rissa appeared at that moment, so he gave Anna a small wave. "I'll see you there. And I promise I'll show up. At some point."

"Thanks again for breakfast. Nice to meet you, Rissa."

The path back to her car was in the opposite direction of the café's windows, but she couldn't stop herself from looking back over her shoulder. And when she saw Finn's face in the window as he watched her walking away, she almost tripped over her own feet.

Why couldn't she have crossed paths with this man in any other place at any other time? Instead, she'd finally met a guy who fascinated her on every level, and he was firmly off-limits. She was lying to him. He was lying to her. Everybody was lying, and a physical relationship with Finn would add a massive knot to the already snarled situation.

Not for the first time, she wondered if he felt bad in any way about lying to her. She thought he probably did, because the more she observed him—especially when he was with Tess—the clearer it became none of this was his idea. And he couldn't confess the truth to Anna. Not at his grandmother's expense.

And she couldn't confess her part in it to him, either. They were stuck in this tangled web that Tess had woven, and there was no way out for either of them.

She needed to focus her attention on the Bayview Inn and on Christine Smith. No more thinking about Finn's abs or how his leg felt against hers or how his eyes crinkled when he smiled.

And she definitely had to stop thinking about kissing him.

"Are you twitting instead of working?"

Finn looked up at Gram, who had her hands

on her hips and was scowling down at him. He'd sat on a bucket of joint compound for maybe two minutes to respond to an important client email, and of course she had to show up during those two minutes.

"It's tweeting, Gram, and no, I'm not on Twitter. Just dealing with some email." He arched an eyebrow. "You know, my *actual* work."

"I think you're supposed to be in the new bathroom."

He nodded. "Probably. I'll be there in a minute."

One of the design changes Anna had suggested was a master suite upstairs. Turning the old den downstairs into a bedroom with a small bathroom for Tess meant she wouldn't have to climb the stairs as often. Taking Tess's room upstairs, along with the other bedroom on the back of the house, and combining them meant there was room for a small bathroom and walk-in closet, but a small sitting area. It meant three guest rooms instead of four, but even Finn understood how much more they'd be able to charge for a suite that didn't require a shared bathroom and offered some private relaxation space.

Not that it mattered, Finn knew, since Gram had about as much chance of working in hospitality as she did of winning the Boston Marathon. Maybe less. He still wasn't sure if she was actually serious about wanting the house to become the Bayview

Inn, but he didn't want to get into it with her right now. They had enough problems in their lives.

Regardless of the house's future use, he liked the idea of Gram's bedroom being downstairs, since that was something he and his parents had been worrying about for a while. They'd even talked to Gram about it a few times, to no avail. He wasn't sure if she just put more stock in Anna's opinion, since she was a professional, or if she'd been worried about the expense of it, especially since behind the fake limps and caftans she was currently showing off, she was pretty hardy for her age and the stairs hadn't been an issue.

Either way, Anna had made it happen, and now Finn was supposed to be installing the new showerhead or something. Or running the pipe for it and then capping it off so they could pressurize the system and check for leaks before moving on to the next project. He wasn't a plumber and he certainly shouldn't be playing one on TV, but he was the only member of the family tall enough to do the work without needing a ladder.

An hour later, he was frustrated, sweating and had a renewed appreciation for the nonfictional version of his life. Sure, he missed living in Blackberry Bay, but right now he missed his desk, business lunches and the solitary crunching of numbers more.

The shower was large, but the bathroom wasn't,

and having Cody and his camera in there, plus Tess "helping," heated the small space in a hurry.

"All I have to do," he muttered under his breath, "is get this cap on here so it doesn't gush out when we turn the water on to test for leaks."

He couldn't get the stupid cap to thread onto the end of the pipe that would eventually join with the showerhead, no matter how much he tried, and his frustration level was steadily rising. It was going to be break time pretty soon, whether the *Relic Rehab* crew liked it or not.

Realistically, they had enough footage of him wrestling with the little metal cap and he was getting ready to tap out and let Frankie or Jim finish the job when he heard a hissing sound that made him freeze.

"Where did Gram go?" he asked just as a flood burst out of the uncapped pipe and doused him in extremely cold water.

He gasped from the shock, then cursed as he tried to find the cap he'd dropped on the shower floor.

"Turn the water off," he shouted, and then he gave up on the cap. If he hadn't been able to tighten it under ideal conditions, he certainly wasn't going to install it while taking an involuntary cold shower.

Alternating between cursing and yelling for somebody to please turn the damn water off, he tried to cover the end of the pipe with his palm and only managed to deflect the water into a spray that went in every direction. Finally, he managed to block the flow with the heel of his hand.

Stuck standing with his arm over his head and water dripping down his face, he yelled to shut off the water one more time, with as much volume as he could muster. Finally he felt the pressure stop and, as his father and Anna pushed into the room, he cautiously moved his hand. The water that had been backed up against it dumped out onto him, but that was the end of it.

He stood in the shower surrounded, sopping wet and not very happy about it, while everybody else in the room laughed.

"Who turned the water on?" he growled.

"Tess said you told her to turn the water on so you could check for leaks," Anna said.

"I was talking to myself, about *when* we turned the water on to check for leaks."

"Oh." Anna looked like the picture of innocence, except for the amusement dancing in her eyes. "That was a miscommunication."

"I don't think we're going to be able to use any of that footage," Cody said.

Finn glared at him and tried, with little success, to keep the growl out of his voice. "I'm not reenacting that."

"Can't you just beep out the bad words?" Joel

asked, his face still red from the exertion of laughing so hard at his son's predicament.

"Sometimes if there's only one, you can't read the person's lips, and the footage is worth it, we'll beep out one word, but our network is really focused on being family friendly. And to be honest, that would probably all blend into one *really* long beep."

"Trust me, there is nothing about me that's family friendly right now," Finn told him.

"Okay, Cody," Anna said, all business again. "I think we're done in here for now. You can go dry your equipment off if it got wet. Luckily the drain caught most of it—what Finn's clothes didn't, anyway—but I'll have to dry this up."

"I'll run to the house and get you a change of clothes," his dad said, and he was gone before Finn could tell him his current plan was to get out of here—get on his bike and drive until the wind had dried him out and maybe improved his mood at the same time.

For a room that had been crammed full of people, it sure emptied out fast, and Finn found himself alone with Anna.

They hadn't been alone since breakfast, when he'd gotten her all to himself. Remembering the way she hadn't pulled back from the heat of his leg against hers and looking at her now changed his mood entirely.

"I think you did this deliberately," he said, fighting to keep from grinning at her.

"Me? I'm not the one who said to turn the water on."

"Maybe your guys gave me a cap that doesn't fit on that piping."

She laughed. "We did *not* sabotage you, although now that I've seen you, I might have if I'd thought of it. But I had nothing to do with this, which is obvious from the fact I'm still dry."

He took a step toward her, challenging her with a grin that gave her plenty of warning that he was up to no good. "Are you being smug right now because you're dry?"

She didn't back up. "Just pointing out that only one of us got himself doused by a cold shower."

"I can fix that, you know."

"You wouldn't dare." She still hadn't backed away, and there was a challenging gleam in her eye that really turned him on.

"Wouldn't I?" He reached out and pulled her into a big bear hug.

She squealed, laughing against his chest, as her clothes absorbed some of the water that saturated his. When she braced her hands against his shoulders, he assumed she intended to push him away, so he dropped his arms. He was playing, not holding her captive.

But she didn't push him away. She ran her hands

over his shoulders and tilted her head back so he could see her face. And what he saw there was an invitation to kiss her.

Finally.

Kissing Anna was everything he'd hoped it would be and more. Her lips were soft against his, and he cupped the back of her neck with one hand. He wanted to run his hands through her hair and feel the long strands tangled in his fingers, but she had her hair up in a ponytail and now wasn't the time to free it.

Instead he explored her mouth, dipping his tongue between her lips. Her fingers gripped his upper arms before sliding back to his shoulders. The tiny moan that escaped her and the way her teeth caught his bottom lip drove him wild inside and he wished they were anywhere but where they were.

Finn reluctantly pulled away when approaching footsteps broke through the haze of desire clouding his brain. Anna took a step back, running her thumb over her bottom lip just as Eryn appeared in the doorway.

Her assistant stopped short and her gaze bounced between them before doing a long sweep of Anna's body that made Finn wince. Anna's clothes were definitely not dry anymore. The front of her clothes, anyway—the side of her that had been pressed up against him.

"I was, uh...helping Finn put the cap on the pipe," Anna said, as if there could be some other explanation for her current state.

"You mean the cap that's on the floor in the corner?"

Anna's cheeks turned a darker shade of pink. "I was going to get it, but I tripped and Finn caught me. You know how clumsy I can be."

"Oh, absolutely," Eryn said, and if Finn was her boss, he'd give her a significant raise based on her ability to keep a straight face alone. "At least it happened at the end of the day and not the beginning."

"Yes," Anna said. "We can head out so I can just change when we get back to the campground. Joel's bringing dry clothes for Finn, and on our way out, I'll tell Frankie to come cap that pipe off."

"If you see my grandmother on your way out, tell her I said thanks so much for the cold shower."

"I guess we'll see you tomorrow," Anna said since there was nothing left to say in front of Eryn, but she looked over her shoulder at him on their way out, and gave him a look that meant there was probably going to be another, more deliberate, cold shower in his future. But with the memory of her mouth against his still fresh in his memory, it was a price he was willing to pay.

Three hours later, he was pretending to look at his laptop while actually planning how he might get Anna alone for some more kissing tomorrow. He was trying not to grin, since his dad had caught him smiling at his screen earlier and he'd had to mutter something about a client's portfolio. It was hard *not* to smile when he thought about kissing her, though.

Then he got a text message from Anna that sent him on a roller-coaster ride from the high of seeing her name in the notification and then plunging to the low of reading what she wrote.

No more kissing. I shouldn't have done that. I have to be professional, so no matter how much I liked kissing you, no more kissing.

At least she'd confessed to liking kissing him. Part of him wanted to send a flirtatious response, such as asking her if that only applied to kissing her on the mouth? Or reminding her there were a lot of ways to touch that didn't involve kissing.

But if she needed to be professional, he had to respect that, so he limited himself to agreeing.

Okay, no more kissing. Let me know if you change your mind.

Chapter Eight

"Hey, Anna, the electrician wants to know if you can meet him for a few minutes this evening. He said there's an ice cream stand with tables next to the town park, about seven o'clock?"

She looked over at Eryn, frowning. "Did he say why?"

"Nope." Her assistant held up her phone to show her the text. Hers was always the number given to the property owners and contractors they hired, since she had a separate, personal cell phone. Anna only had the one and didn't like giving out the number. Then Eryn moved closer to Anna so she could keep her voice low. "Maybe there's a problem and he doesn't want to talk to you about it with the family around."

Apprehension made Anna's skin prickle. What if the electrician was having some kind of crisis of conscience and wanted to confess that the whole Bayview Inn thing was a fraud? "Tell him I'll be there."

She knew it was going to cause her some anxiety for the rest of the day, but there wasn't much she could do about it. If Brady did try to tell her Tess was lying about the house's history, she might be able to shrug it off. She could tell him that some properties were more historical than others, but that the house and location were too beautiful to pass up. And she *had* learned from Joel that his great-great-great-grandfather had built the house. It was a historical family home. It just wasn't an inn and never had been. If Brady wanted to reveal something about Tess being a fraud, she'd just have to get him on board as far as continuing to go along with the story.

Shortly after their lunch break, Anna filmed some segments in the guest rooms upstairs with Mike while Eryn and Cody were with the family downstairs. Basically just her walking through the rooms and giving a recap of what they'd done and what they were hoping to accomplish. She kept it short and simple, since she already knew they wouldn't need filler for the Bayview Inn episodes.

Once they were done, she lingered in the room. It looked out over the back of the property, and she had to admit that given her age, Tess kept some incredible gardens. A lot of the beds were perennials and wildflowers, but they were beautiful riots of color and free of weeds. Considering how early it was in the season, a lot of thought had obviously gone into the planning.

She heard footsteps enter the room and turned, expecting Mike or Eryn. But it was Finn, and he stopped short when he saw her. "I didn't know you were in here. Hope I'm not interrupting."

It was three days since he'd kissed her. Or she'd kissed him. The only thing she knew for sure was that she had enjoyed that kiss thoroughly, and it was probably for the best that they hadn't been alone since.

No more kissing. Possibly the rashest words she'd ever sent in a text message, and she wished she could take them back. It wouldn't be smart on her part, but depriving herself of this man's kisses—and possibly more—for the duration of her stay in town didn't feel like a smart decision, either.

"Just going over my to-do list in my head," she said, since telling him she was spending her alone time worrying about an off-site meeting with the electrician would only lead to questions she didn't have the answers to. And probably wouldn't want to give him if she did.

"We're looking for my dad's phone."

She smiled. "I guess you've already tried calling it?"

"Yeah, but he silences it so it doesn't go off while the cameras are on, and it's not vibrating enough to be found. Its last known location is in this house, but that's not super helpful."

"I don't think I've seen it," she said. "But I know Mike and Cody had a pile of tech stuff on the kitchen counter. It might have gotten tossed in with that accidentally."

"Thanks." He started to leave but turned back to face her. "Are you okay? You seem a little... I don't know. Sad? Upset?"

"I'm fine. It's been a long day, I guess."

"You're sure?" he asked, the warmth in his eyes making her feel all sorts of things she didn't want to be feeling.

Please just go.

Please come over here and kiss me again.

"I'm sure."

"Okay. Let me know if you need anything, though." And then he was gone, leaving her staring at the empty doorway and thinking she could really use a hug. Among other things, of course, but right now the thought of his strong arms wrapped around her and holding her close almost brought tears to her eyes.

After shaking off the melancholy, she got back to work. They were going to tackle the kitchen very soon and though the room didn't allow for a lot of flexibility in design, she wanted to have plenty of notes to go over with Tess. They'd have a one-on-one meeting—or one-on-four, actually, since the rest of the family wasn't going to let Tess make design choices unattended, thanks to the salmon pink—within the next couple of days, and it would be tight filming since they'd have both cameras in the kitchen with them.

She took measurements and made sketches until it was time to call it quits, and then she ate a light dinner with Eryn and the crew. The big RV had an outdoor kitchen and they grilled some chicken breasts while Mike made what he called a garden salad but was really a pile of tomatoes, shredded cheese and croutons, with just enough cucumber and lettuce to make it respectable.

When the alert went off on her watch, she went to her RV to freshen up and grab the car keys. Even though she hadn't eaten much, her stomach was tied up in such a knot of nerves that it almost ached. After brushing her teeth and redoing her ponytail, she grabbed her bag and stepped back outside.

Eryn was waiting for her. "Are you sure you don't want me to go with you?"

"I'm sure." She couldn't take the chance the electrician wanted to expose the scam Tess was running, and this was about the time of day Eryn usually called her wife. "I'll probably only be a few minutes, and you know you want to FaceTime Kelly before the baby goes down for the night."

"It just seems a little off," Eryn said, her eyebrows drawn together in an impressive scowl. If she only knew just how *off* everything really was.

"We've already met the electrician. And we're meeting in a very public place. Go make your call and I'll probably be back before you're done."

Her confidence faded as soon as she was in the car, and her hands trembled as she gripped the steering wheel. She couldn't take Eryn with her. Or any of the guys, for that matter. She couldn't take that chance without knowing what was on Brady's mind. But it *was* odd that he hadn't just stopped by the house to talk to her.

When she reached the ice cream shop, she didn't see him anywhere, so she bought a soda and a small dish of twist with jimmies and sat at one of the small wrought iron patio sets between the shop and the park. She wasn't sure she even wanted the ice cream, but this was where she'd agreed to meet and it would have felt strange to sit at one of their tables without buying one.

She'd eaten about half of it and abandoned the spoon in the rapidly melting ice cream when he finally approached the table. "Anna? Brady Nash. We met briefly at Tess's the other day, but it was pretty busy and I wasn't sure you'd remember."

"I remember, and it's good to see you again," she said, deliberately keeping her tone light so he wouldn't see her underlying tension. "Please, join me."

After pulling out the chair across from her, he sat and folded his hands on the wrought iron table-top. "You scored a table in the shade. Well done."

"Do you want an ice cream?" She gestured at hers with her spoon. "It's good. I would have gotten two, but I wasn't sure what flavor to get."

He smiled, and something in his eyes set off alarm bells, though she couldn't say why. There was something vaguely familiar about his face, but she couldn't put her finger on it. "I'm all set, thanks. When I leave, I'm going to grab some to take home to Reyna—my wife."

"Reyna." Anna tilted her head. "She and her mom own the combination car repair shop and bakery?"

"That's her." He practically glowed when he said it, and Anna felt a pang of jealousy. She wouldn't mind having a man look that proud when he talked about her. "She's probably already getting text messages from people speculating about why her husband is having ice cream with the pretty out-of-towner from the TV show."

"Gossipy town, huh?" Luckily, the inn was a big enough project to exhaust her crew, so they were mostly traveling between the campground and the house, without spending a lot of time in town.

"Like you wouldn't believe."

"So what can I do for you, Brady?" It was time to cut to the chase. "My assistant told me you didn't really say."

He was silent for so long she had time to register the ticking sound wasn't in her head and that there was a real, old-fashioned pedestal clock with a second hand standing a few feet away.

"I'm pretty sure you're my sister," he finally said in a voice that was very low and suddenly sounded very rough.

Tick. Tick. Tick.

After finally remembering to swallow and finding it difficult, Anna took a sip of her soda to wet her dry mouth. Her mind was reeling, but she had to say something. Anything. "So the people speculating that this meeting might be gossip worth reporting to your wife either don't know I'm your sister, or they have seriously twisted imaginations."

"Mom, my brother, Chris, and our wives are the only people who even know I *have* a sister." *Mom.* She must have made a face because he winced.

"Christy. My moth…*our* mother, I guess. If I'm right."

"You're right," she whispered.

Christy. Christine Elizabeth Smith… Nash. Anna hadn't known she went by Christy. When her dad had broken the news of her biological mother to her, that was exactly how he'd referred to her. *Your mother*. He hadn't even called her by her name, never mind a nickname. She'd found that out when she was finally given the birth certificate she'd never seen before.

"I've only known since a few days before Christmas," he continued, keeping his voice low, though the rough edges had smoothed out. "She had some dental surgery and the drugs made her loopy. She told me enough to make me ask more questions when the drugs wore off."

"What did she tell you?"

"Honestly, not much. Your name and that you were on TV, but when we asked her more questions, she dug in her heels. She said she was ashamed and didn't want to talk about it. And that she checked on you once, but your father told her you were happy and healthy and loved the woman he'd married as if she was your own mom. She didn't want us turning your life upside down."

Heat flooded Anna's face and her fingers curled until her nails were pressing into her palms. "She was ashamed."

Brady started to reach across the table, as though to comfort her, but froze just shy of touching her arm. After a few seconds, he pulled his hand back. "Not of you. She was ashamed of herself, because she left you."

Then why didn't she come back? Anna didn't voice the question because she wasn't sure she could just ask it. She was afraid if she finally asked the question that had haunted her since she was sixteen, it would be at full wail and within minutes, everybody in town would be talking about her.

But Brady—*holy crap, her brother*—must have run out of bombs to drop because he was just watching her, waiting for her to say something. After mentally shoving back The Big Question, she realized she did have others.

"Is she married? Who's your dad?" She stopped for a second, blinking. "Are there more brothers or sisters?"

"It's just Chris and I, although I guess I could have other siblings out there, but I wouldn't have any way to know since my father never looked back after he left us."

He said it matter-of-factly enough, so maybe it was her own issues when it came to an absent parent that had her looking for the tightness around his mouth and tension in his shoulders.

"So I got the dad and no mom, and you got the

mom but no dad," she said softly, even though it wasn't really true. She'd had a mother. Just not the mother she'd been born to.

"Chris and I are both married. His wife teaches school and they have two boys—CJ and Benny. And my wife, Reyna, and I have a little guy named Parker who's almost eleven months old."

Anna's head spun as she absorbed the information. There was this entire family she belonged to, yet didn't even know. "I have two half sisters, from my dad. And I was married once. I'm divorced now."

"When I heard you were in town, I did a Google search. I'm sorry your divorce went down like that."

Anna's face flamed, as it always did when she thought about her ex-husband. Finding out about his infidelity when her phone blew up with texts from friends with a link to the tabloid photos had been so traumatizing that she still wanted to curl up in a ball when reminded of those dark days. But a more relevant thought pushed its way through the lingering humiliation. "How did you know who I am?"

"You look like her," he said bluntly. "From when I was a kid."

"People keep asking me if they've met me before, so I figured there had to be a resemblance."

"A very strong resemblance. Remarkable, really.

When I first saw you at Tess's house, you were on the phone. The way you looked and sounded in that moment—even the way you were standing—was like the strongest déjà vu I've ever experienced. Add in the fact I knew you had a TV show and she told us your first name." He shrugged. "I just knew, I guess."

"Who else knows?" she asked in barely more than a whisper because it was so hard to force the words out. "That I'm here, I mean."

"Right now, as far as I know, I'm the only person who knows. I was going to tell Mom because there's this part of her heart that's broken by what she did, but…" He paused for a few seconds, shaking his head. "But as much as I'd hate keeping this big a secret from her, it's really your choice if you want to meet her or not."

Meet her. Anna's hands trembled and she clasped them in her lap. "She still lives here? Or close by?"

"She lives here in Blackberry Bay. She came back after…well, after she left you and your dad. Nobody in town ever knew she'd had a baby while she was away. But I figure you either came here looking for her or this is the world's most wild coincidence."

"A little of both, actually. The Bayview Inn application was a coincidence. But when I chose it, I was hoping to get to know more about her."

"Well, you can actually get to know *her*. But only if you want to."

A chill went down Anna's spine, making her shiver despite the warmth of the evening. "I... don't know."

She'd expected—*hoped*—to learn more about the woman who'd abandoned her to her father. But somehow she'd never considered the possibility she might actually be able to meet her mother. The show getting an application from the town where her mother had been born decades before had seemed an unlikely coincidence. Her mother still living there had seemed too far-fetched to even consider.

"You don't have to decide right now," Brady said. "I'm not going to tell anybody—well, except Reyna, because spousal privileges and all that. And I know Tess's house well enough to know you're not leaving anytime soon. Your assistant has my contact info, so just reach out if you decide you want to meet her. Or just...to keep in touch with me, if you want."

"I go out for ice cream and get an instant brother," she said with a chuckle.

"I've known I have a sister a little longer than you've known you have two brothers, so I'm not going to push. But no matter what you decide about our mother, I'd love to have you over to the house to spend time with me and my family before you leave town."

She nodded, unexpected tears welling up in her eyes. "I'm an aunt."

"Three instant nephews." He blew out a breath. "I do hope you'll at least meet her. I think it would bring both of you some peace. And Parker's not really talking yet, but at some point Auntie Anna might get mentioned."

"Give me a few days to think about it," she said, though she already knew she wasn't going to be able to leave town without at least meeting Christy. Especially since keeping in touch with her nephews was already feeling important to her.

"No pressure," he said, giving her a warm smile before he pushed back his chair and stood. "I should grab that ice cream and get home, but you can call or text me anytime."

She stood and reached out to shake his hand. Somehow a hug felt more like the thing to do, but there were people around and that would be a lot harder to explain. "I'll shoot you a text later so you'll have my number instead of going through Eryn."

"Perfect. And listen, this town is fueled by gossip, like I said before, and more than a few people might try to ferret out why you and I were seen having a conversation today, but nobody needs to know the truth. Just tell them you had some questions about the electrical work I've done at the house—at the inn, I mean—because everybody knows I've spent years trying to keep that woman from burning the place down with antique extension cords."

Anna blinked. "That's right. You're Finn's friend."

"Yeah, we go way back." He held up his phone. "Let me know what you decide, okay?"

She nodded and then watched him walk away, wondering if she should call him back and make him swear on whatever she could come up with that he wouldn't tell Finn she was Christy Nash's daughter.

What a tangled web she'd managed to get herself wrapped up in.

It had been about eighteen hours since Finn walked into the upstairs bedroom and found Anna alone. And he'd spent every one of those eighteen hours regretting not kissing her again. Except for the hours he'd been asleep, of course. Hours during which he'd had a dream he really wished hadn't faded from his mind within minutes of waking up.

No more kissing.

He'd respect her decision, of course, but he was grumpy about it. And having spent the morning with his entire family and the whole *Relic Rehab* crew in the kitchen—which had felt a lot smaller than it usually did—arguing over the best way to renovate it certainly hadn't helped his mood. They'd spent a solid twenty minutes just convincing Gram she didn't need an espresso-and-latte-making station.

"People like those sorts of drinks," she'd said, putting her family in the unpleasant position of not being able to point out there *were* no people. They'd had to rely on Anna trying to make her understand there really wasn't space for it and that regular coffee was fine in the mornings.

And Finn had almost choked on the water he was drinking when Gram essentially confirmed she was actually planning to keep this ridiculousness going by actually making the house an inn. He'd really been hoping her comments to that effect had simply been to support the renovation scheme, but if she was going to try to make the house pay for itself by inviting strangers to stay in it, there were going to be a *lot* of phone calls from his mother in his future. They were going to need a better plan.

Now that everybody had scattered to other parts of the house—probably all needing a break from each other—he was alone in the kitchen, taking the cabinet doors off and other mindless tasks that gave him an excuse to not be a part of whatever else was going on.

When Anna walked in, notebook in hand and frowning in concentration, he had mixed feelings about the interruption. He wasn't thrilled about giving up his alone time. But, on the other hand, he did like seeing her walk into a room.

She'd been out of sorts today, though. Just as she'd been toward the end of yesterday. Distracted, as though she was lost in thought when she was usually focused on every detail of what they were doing. And he wasn't sure if it was the kiss, or something else. Or maybe Gram or one of his parents had let something slip—said something that wasn't adding up when it came to the falsified history of the inn. That possibility kept him from coming right out and asking her if anything was bothering her.

"I need to make a run to the hardware store," Anna said as she tore the sheet out of her notebook.

Finn wasn't sure if she was talking to him or to herself, but he wasn't thrilled with the idea of her going to the hardware store alone. While Gram might think she had everybody on board with her plan, Albert Foss was definitely a wild card. "We can take a short road trip in my dad's truck if you want. Hit the big-box store."

"I don't need *that* much. And I like small-town hardware stores. They usually have decades' worth of cool stuff to pick through. You never know what you're going to find." She looked at him thoughtfully. "But I wouldn't turn down a ride, if you're offering. It won't fit in the car, and the crew is in and out of the SUV all day. They use the back like a mobile storage closet."

"Whenever you're ready." Being alone with her was going to cause all sorts of problems with his willpower, but her being alone with Albert at the hardware store could cause even worse problems.

"Five minutes?" she asked after a glance at her watch. "I just want to ask the others if they can think of anything else we need right now."

That gave him five minutes to give himself a stern talking to. This wasn't a date. They weren't going cruising down a back road. They weren't parking by the lake and making out as best they could in the bucket front seats of his pickup. It was a quick errand and he was going to be all business. Drive her to the hardware store. Help her find the stuff she needed. Load it in the bed of the truck. That was it.

No more kissing.

When she walked out of the house almost ten minutes letter, her cheeks flushed with what looked like a mix of exasperation and heat, that resolve slipped a little. She wasn't a great actress. He knew he could get her to rescind her no-kissing rule with very little effort on his part.

But he wouldn't, because that would make him a jerk. She'd given him her boundaries and he would abide by them.

She was quiet during the ride, her gaze alternating between the passing scenery and the list in her hand. Her head moved slightly in time to the radio, so he just let her enjoy the music while he navigated the narrow streets, looking for a place to park near the hardware store.

"This town seems to get busier every day," she said as he turned the ignition off. She handed him the list to hold while she unbuckled and sorted her bag and her phone before getting out of the truck.

"It's the Friday of Memorial Day weekend," he pointed out. "Tourists are good for our economy, but not great for parking. It gets worse when schools let out for the summer, and between July Fourth and Labor Day, most of the people who live here just walk or do their errands on Tuesdays and Wednesdays."

After pulling open the hardware store's wooden screen door for her, he took a deep breath and followed her inside. This had the potential to be a very bad day.

"Looking for anything in particular?" Albert asked in his standard, gravelly-voiced greeting.

"I have a list of things," Anna said, "but I'd rather just look around for a while. I love hardware stores.

"You look familiar," he said, scowling heavily as he tried to place her.

"Just one of those faces," she said lightly. "I get that a lot. Finn, do you have the list?"

"Right here," he said, holding up the sheet of paper. "Let's start at the back of the store."

"You need any help finding something, just give a shout. Though Finn probably knows where everything is, since his family's had an account here since my grandpa first opened the doors."

"So much history," she said, and Finn bit back a growl. The last thing he needed was for Albert to start talking. He talked entirely too much. "But this will all be going on my company card, since it's for the Bayview Inn project."

"The what?" When Finn gave him a very pointed, wide-eyed look over Anna's head, Albert sighed and folded his beefy arms across his chest. "Right. The inn."

"Should we pick up some more caulking while we're here?" he asked Anna. Anything to steer her away from the conversation and back onto their task. "You can never have too much caulking."

"Yes, you actually can have too much caulking."

To Finn's relief, she took the list out of his hand and started walking toward the back of the store. He shot Albert a final warning look and then followed her down the aisle.

Sometime in the early 1970s, Albert and Finn's grandfather had had a falling out. Gramps had been the road agent at the time, and Albert felt that when snow got plowed, extra was being deposited at the end of his driveway deliberately because the cherry pie Albert's wife had made beat out Gram's for a blue ribbon at Old Home Day. So in retaliation, Albert started a rumor that Tess Weaver made her pie with canned filling, and the next time it snowed, Gramps had spent hours using the town's plow truck to build a veritable mountain of snow across Albert's driveway.

You didn't slander a woman's pie recipe in Blackberry Bay.

Blowing the whistle on Tess Weaver's big scheme would be quite the payback, decades in the making, so Finn didn't breathe an easy breath until Albert had added up all their purchases and handed Anna her credit card back.

But on his last trip out the door with the supplies, Albert called him over. "Hey, Finn. You tell Tess I haven't had a decent cherry pie since my wife passed on. Sure would be nice of her to make me one, even if it *is* second-best."

"I'll give her the message," Finn promised, and then he got the hell out of there before Albert changed his mind.

Or before he really threw caution to the wind and let Albert know in no uncertain terms that nobody in this town currently baked or had *ever* baked a better made-from-scratch cherry pie than Tess Weaver.

Chapter Nine

"Are you sure about this? I feel like if I hit a bump too hard, you might shatter into a bunch of pieces."

Anna inhaled deeply, trying to force her body to relax before turning to look at Brady, who was driving. "I'm not totally sure, but I'm mostly sure. I guess that's as good as it gets when it comes to this sort of thing."

Maybe it was the fact it had been a week since her trip to the hardware store with Finn, who had left town shortly after to avoid the tourists, or so he'd said. But he hadn't come back when they resumed filming on Tuesday, and Alice had only told her something had come up, but that he would be back as soon as he could.

A week without Finn to distract her had opened the door for the realization she'd been in Blackberry Bay for over three weeks and there was an expiration date on her time here. She'd come here to learn more about her mother, and the best way to do that was probably to talk to her. Before she could talk herself out of it, she'd texted Brady.

Now it was a beautiful Saturday afternoon and the brother she'd just met was driving her to the house he'd grown up in so she could meet their mother. It was a lot to wrap her head around.

When the very long driveway ended in front of a small house in a clearing, she told herself it would all be okay. If it didn't go well, she trusted Brady to drive her out of here, no questions asked, as he'd promised he would. And she was going to get a few of her own questions answered.

When the wooden screen door pushed open and two yellow Labs ran out, Anna found herself smiling. Dogs always helped.

"That would be Taffy and Bean," Brady said as he opened his door. "They love absolutely everybody and will try to get you to throw sticks, but once you start, they won't want you to stop."

She ruffled their fur, laughing as they pushed at each other, each trying to be the one to get all the love from the stranger. But when she straightened and looked at the woman who'd just stepped out onto the porch, the laughter stopped abruptly.

No wonder the people in town had been doing double takes since she arrived. If Anna took a Snapchat selfie and one of the lens options aged her around twenty years, the result would be the woman standing in front of her.

"Anna." It was just her name. One word. But coming from her mother's lips, it crashed into Anna and sent her mentally reeling from the impact. "You found me."

Inside Anna's head was a swirling hurricane of thoughts and emotions, but her mother's words triggered the storm surge of anger. "I *found* you? Were you just hanging out here, living your life and waiting for me to show up? Sorry to take so long, but I didn't actually know you existed until I was a teenager, and then I was a little busy."

Christy flinched, but her voice was low and calm. "Can we sit here on the porch and talk?"

Anna wanted to reject her—to give her a *hell no* and walk away, just as this woman had when she was an infant. It was what she deserved.

But some part of her that was still rational knew this was the moment she'd come here for. Finding her mother was why she'd come to Blackberry Bay and was humoring the Weaver family as they tried to scam her.

She'd been looking for information. And after

talking to Brady, she thought she'd prepared her-self for coming face-to-face with her mother. It hadn't helped. There was no way to prepare her-self in advance for this, but if she backed out now, she'd probably never try again.

"I'm sorry," Anna said softly. "I was sixteen when I found out Naomi—my dad's ex-wife—isn't my biological mother. I think that was my inner teenager lashing out."

"I understand. I really do."

When Anna took a step toward the porch, Brady touched her arm. "I'm going to take the dogs around back. If you want to go, just call for me and we'll go."

She nodded and then sat in one of the rocking chairs Christy gestured to before sitting in one a respectful distance away.

"How much has your father told you?" Christy asked softly.

"Not much. He doesn't really like to talk about you."

"I guess I can't blame him for that."

Anna made a sound of disbelief. "You guess? You left him with an infant and never looked back."

"I looked back," she said softly. "But it was too late."

"I don't have children," Anna said. "But if I did,

I don't think there would ever be a *too late* when it came to them."

"I think every mother wants to believe that." There was so much sorrow in Christy's eyes that Anna had to look away. "I drank a lot before I had you. And I drank even more after. Now I recognize that I suffered from postpartum depression, but at the time, I was just exhausted and failing and I drank. A lot. That's not an excuse. Just a reason. But I was not only toxic, you weren't safe with me, and I had just enough lucidity to recognize that, so I left."

She wasn't safe with her? "What did my dad do?"

"We were young, Anna. So young. And he knew I was unhappy and drinking too much, but we'd fight about it and then he'd leave. He had to work two jobs, so I'm not sure he knew just how bad off I was."

"He didn't know I wasn't safe with you?" That was hard for her to wrap her head around. Outside of the lie that had tainted their relationship for a long time, she'd always considered herself lucky to have such a loving dad.

Christy leaned forward in her chair, her body language showing her sense of urgency. "I never hurt you. I swear I didn't. I just…there were always these thoughts in my head. That I *might* hurt you, and that you'd be better off without me. But it was the thoughts that I should spare *you* from a life of hardship that really scared me. That's when I left."

Anna forced herself to meet Christy's gaze, and she could see the pain in her mother's eyes. She didn't even want to imagine how lost and terrified Christy must have felt, and she felt empathy swelling inside of her. If she'd been in that dark a place, she probably *did* believe abandoning her daughter was the best thing she could do for her.

"I wasn't worth the effort of getting help?" Anna asked, and she was surprised by how small and needy her voice sounded.

"I thought I was beyond help," Christy said, looking directly into Anna's eyes. "We had no money. Our relationship was awful—he changed when we had you, and I didn't. I was an alcoholic. And I didn't have the first idea of how to find resources. I just knew in my heart that you would be safer without me."

Anna remembered when her youngest sister was born. Naomi had struggled so badly, and that was with the care and support of her family and with financial resources. Naomi was a wonderful mother, and trying to imagine how her and her children's lives would have turned out had she been an alcoholic going through postpartum depression without any love or support broke Anna's heart.

"And when you got better?" she asked in a softer voice.

"You were two when I reached out to your father, and he…he gave me pictures of you with the woman he'd married. He said you believed she was your mother, and I could see the love between you two in the photographs. He also said he'd fight to protect you, and I was sober, but still a little shaky. I had nothing to speak of. Nothing to offer you. I couldn't afford a lawyer and, even if I could, I thought a custody battle would harm both of us—your happiness and my sobriety. You were happy and healthy and safe and… I let you go."

Anna was trembling, and she folded her hands in her lap. Maybe to hide it, or maybe just to give herself something to look at while she tried to process what she was feeling.

"I regret not getting to be a part of your life," Christy continued. "But I don't regret leaving. I'm sorry you found out about me the way you did, but that wasn't my choice. Your father and I each did what we thought was best for you."

The direct way she said it, along with the sincerity Anna could feel with every fiber of her being, caused her eyes to well up, and one tear slid over her cheek before she could swipe them away.

Would her life have been different if her father had let her grow up knowing that Naomi was her stepmother? He could have told her that her birth mother had been unwell, and maybe he could have left the door open for her to get to know Christy.

She would have at least *known* and not had that bomb dropped on her during her sophomore year in high school, which was no picnic for anybody, while her parents were going through a divorce.

She knew she should say something. Christy had opened herself up and tried to be honest about the mother she had been and why she'd done what she had—which was leaving her daughter to be raised by two parents who loved her very much. Her issues with her dad not telling her the truth weren't Christy's fault.

"I'm not going to push," Christy said softly. "I want you to know that I have loved you every day of your life and if this moment is all I have of you, I will treasure this memory and be thankful for it. I understand that. But, after you've had some time, I would love to see you again while you're in town."

Anna looked up into the face that was so much like hers and was surprised to find herself smiling. "It's a lot to process."

"I can't imagine how you feel. Now that we've done this hardest part, if you want Brady to take you home, you can process how you feel and maybe we can get together again. We could have lunch here, or maybe dinner at Chris's house, all together."

Anna's instinct was to nod, so she went with her gut. "I think I'd like that."

"And I'm a very private person and my boys

respect that—and you—so we'll keep our family business to ourselves."

"That might prove difficult since everybody in this town sees the resemblance, even if they can't quite put the puzzle pieces together." She stood as she said it, and Christy let out a whistle as she got to her feet.

"This town," she said, shaking her head. "You're right. If we were to meet in town, there would be no putting that horse back in the barn."

Taffy and Bean ran around the corner of the house and up the porch to get love first from Christy, and then Anna. Brady was right behind them.

"I'll come back and throw sticks for you another time, okay?" Anna said to the dogs, scratching their heads, and she heard Christy's tremulous sigh of relief.

It was time to leave and Anna felt herself tense when Christy took a small step forward. She wasn't sure hugging was on the table quite yet.

But Christy put out her hand, and when Anna took it, she covered it with her other hand. "Thank you for coming today, Anna."

"I'll see you again," she said, because she knew it was true. This time with Christy was already helping to heal the hurts Anna had been holding in her heart since she was sixteen, and while Naomi was always going to be her mother, she wanted to make room in her life for Christy.

She and Brady were both quiet during the drive back to where she'd left her car, but it wasn't a tense silence. It was more like he recognized that she had a lot of emotions running amok inside, and he was giving her the space she needed.

"How is Chris doing with all of this?" she asked about the brother she'd yet to meet, as Brady pulled up beside her car.

"He'd like to meet you. He's worried about Mom, of course. Not to in any way take away from what you're going through, but it's a lot for her, too."

"Maybe we could all get together at some point. Not like *right now*, but soon."

He nodded. "We all get together at Chris's for dinner a lot, usually on Friday nights. I'll send you a text message next time and if you're ready, you can join us. If you're not ready yet, I'll let you know the next time."

"Thanks. And thanks for today. For everything, really."

"Hey, what are brothers for?" he asked, nudging her with his elbow.

Anna laughed, and she was still smiling when she got in her car to drive back to the campground. But, just because she didn't have enough coincidences happening in her life, she got a text

message from her dad just as she parked next to
the RV.

I haven't heard from you for a while. Where are you?

Sorry, I was busy sitting on my birth mother's
front porch. She typed the words to make herself
feel better, but then she deleted them. I'm on location. Things are hectic, but I'll call you tomorrow.

Then she accidentally slammed the RV door
too hard, startling Eryn, who'd been watching a
video on her phone.

"Sorry," she said. "I didn't mean to close it that
hard."

"Anna, are you okay?" Eryn actually set her
phone on the table, which meant she was worried.
"You've been in kind of a weird mood lately."

"I think it's time to find a place to have a drink
in this town."

"There's a place that attracts more locals than
tourists that's called The Dock. I guess it has a
dock." She shrugged. "So it depends on whether
we want to sit and sip a glass of wine or if we're
in a head-down-to-the-docks-and-kick-back kind
of mood."

The *we* gave Anna a moment of pause because
she wasn't sure her assistant, alcohol and a bunch
of people who knew the truth about the Bayview

Inn were a good mix, but she was not in the mood
to sip a glass of wine.

"Let's go kick back."

Finn had only been sitting at the bar for about
three minutes when he heard her laugh.

Anna.

He hadn't seen her for a week, but he didn't
even have to turn around to know it was her. Other
than closing his eyes for a moment, allowing himself to savor the sound, he gave no indication he'd
heard her. His dad was sitting on the stool next to
him, and the last thing Joel wanted right now was
more *Relic Rehab* in his life.

After spending the week putting out a few fires
with Tom—stuff that really needed them side-by-
side in the office—Finn had arrived back in Blackberry Bay to find his father sitting on the front step
of the house, looking as though he'd been through
a commercial washer and dryer. Twice.

Apparently his father's life had become nothing
but his wife complaining to him about his mother,
and his mother complaining to him about his wife.
He'd been sitting on the front step, trying to figure out some place to go that wasn't back inside
his house, when Finn pulled into the driveway.

He'd parked the bike and then they'd gotten in his
dad's truck and off they'd gone in search of a beer.

Maybe a guys' night out would help with his

dad's woman troubles, but being in a bar, listening to the woman he wanted laughing and having a good time while he had to sit with his back to her was going to be hell on Finn.

By shifting slightly to his left, he could see her reflection in the giant mirror with some kind of alcohol advertisement etched on it. She was with Eryn and a woman he didn't recognize. Their companion was dressed like a tourist, though, so maybe they'd made friends with a woman who'd been there solo.

While his dad vented about life with Alice and Tess, most of which Finn had already heard about or had actually been present for, Finn kept part of his attention on Anna.

And when she got up and went down the hall to the restrooms, he told his dad he'd be right back and followed her. It wasn't one of his prouder moments, but he wanted a chance to have a moment alone with her. The hallway led to a small room with a restroom on each end and a couple of benches, because sometimes there was a line. Tonight there wasn't, though.

When she came out of the ladies' room and saw him, her eyes widened and then she smiled. "You came back."

"Of course I did. You look like you're having fun tonight." She nodded, and at the same time she was walking toward him. He ended up with his back against the wall and Anna very close to him. He didn't mind. "Is Eryn drinking, too?"

She held up one finger. "One drink. That's all she ever has and then she has soda water with lemon."

"Good. How many have you had?" he teased, making her roll her eyes.

"Three. I had a lot going on today, though, and I forgot to eat, so maybe I should have had two."

And one of the reasons The Dock was so popular with the locals, even though they had to put up with the tourists who wanted to eat on the actual dock, was the fact they did *not* mix a weak drink.

"I just wanted to make sure one of you was okay to drive back to the campground," he said. "Obviously that would be Eryn."

"You need to get some Uber going in this town," she said, poking her finger at his chest.

"We had a couple of guys try it, but with the traffic it was faster for people to walk, and eventually they gave up. Ricky keeps an eye on people and more than once he's had whoever's washing dishes give a customer a ride home."

"I don't want to talk about Ricky anymore," she said, and neither did he, because that finger she'd poked at his chest was now trailing down his sternum in a very suggestive way.

"What do you want to talk about?" It was only a matter of time before somebody came around the corner looking to use the restroom, so he hoped she didn't take too long about it.

"Look. I wanna have sex with you." She braced her hand against the wall, and he wasn't sure if she was trying to look sexy or trying not to fall over. "And I'm pretty sure you wanna have sex with me."

He was pretty sure he did, too. But rather than jump in and confirm it, he decided to let her run with the conversation just to see where it went.

"There's a problem, though," she continued. "I share my RV with Eryn and that would maybe be awkward."

Maybe? It would *definitely* be awkward, which meant they really had two problems. The first being the alcohol. He didn't know her well enough to know how she held her booze, but it seemed like she'd gone at least one drink past knowing or caring what she might regret in the morning. And the second being the RV. "I'm currently staying with my parents, which I think would be even more awkward."

"I don't want anybody to know," she whispered, tilting her head to look past him as though she were about to whisper national security secrets in his ear.

At this point, he didn't care what she whispered in his ear. He just wanted to feel her breath on his skin.

"We could rent a hotel room," she continued in

the same whisper. "Or a suite. With a hot tub. That place with the fancy pool looks nice."

Hell yes, his body responded, but he forced himself to shake his head. "If you don't want anybody to know we're renting a suite together, then renting a suite anywhere in this town is a bad idea."

She frowned, chewing on her bottom lip as she tried to come up with another solution. He tried not to watch. "Maybe I can send Eryn on an errand to…do something important and I'll have the motor home to myself for a few minutes."

If and when Finn finally got Anna naked, he was going to keep her that way for more than a few minutes. "I'll tell you what. Tomorrow, when you're sober, think about it and if, come Monday, you tell me you still want to have sex with me, I'll figure out how to get it done."

"I'll probably still want to."

"Probably?"

She smiled and he almost wished he wasn't such a decent guy so he could suggest they ditch their drinking buddies and make use of his back seat. But he was, so no matter what she said or did, his pants were staying zipped tonight.

"I've wanted to have sex with you every day since I got here," she admitted, and a quiet groan escaped him. "So I'll probably still want to on Monday."

"This might be the first time in my life I've ever looked forward to a Monday."

She hooked her finger over the waistband of his jeans and tugged him even closer. "I changed my mind about the no-kissing thing. You should definitely kiss me."

Between the state she was in and his self-control being on the ragged edge, there was no telling what would happen if he kissed her right now. There was a good chance whatever happened would be talked about in Blackberry Bay for years to come, so he forced himself to put his hands on her shoulders and gently push her upright.

"I'll kiss you on Monday if you still want me to. You should go back to Eryn now, though. She's probably going to come looking for you."

"Okay, but don't forget to kiss me on Monday." And then she was gone.

Since he needed to give her a head start anyway, Finn went into the men's room and splashed some cold water on his face, which was the closest he could get to a cold shower at the moment.

Tomorrow was going to be the longest-feeling Sunday he'd ever experienced.

Chapter Ten

Anna slept in on Sunday, but still woke with a headache and barely enough energy to do more than get out of bed, shower, and go back to bed with her iPad. She watched episode after episode of a cooking show she didn't care about, just to give her mind something to focus on besides Finn.

She'd told him she wanted to have sex with him. Just flat-out said it.

The memory of cornering him outside the restroom made her want to pull the covers up over her head and never come out. But that wouldn't work because Eryn would find her pretty quickly.

Eryn.

She couldn't juggle the Bayview Inn, her

mother *and* Finn without Eryn catching on. Her assistant knew her too well. They shared a living space. They even shared a car. And in a town like Blackberry Bay, it was only natural she'd wonder where Anna was disappearing to. And Anna couldn't come up with any answers that didn't reveal things she'd rather keep to herself.

One thing she knew she didn't want happening was Eryn joining the entire crew in wondering what was going on with Anna.

Turning off her iPad, she got out of bed before she could change her mind. She found Eryn sitting outside in a folding camp chair, reading a paperback thriller. "Hey, Eryn, you got a second?"

"Inside?"

As nice as the weather was outside, she wanted privacy. And the bright sunshine was also killing her head. "Please."

Once Eryn was inside, Anna grabbed them each a water from the fridge and they sat opposite each other at the dinette. Eryn opened her notebook, which she always did when they were going to talk about something work-related, but she definitely wasn't going to need it for this conversation.

"I have something I need to confess to you," Anna said, "but you absolutely can't tell anybody."

"You're banging Finn Weaver."

Anna almost choked on her water. Part of Eryn's job was summarizing information and boiling it down to the pertinent details for her boss, and clearly she deserved a raise. "No, that's...okay, yes. Not yet. But I will be."

There wasn't much sense in denying that one.

"Honestly," Eryn said, "when I saw him go down the hallway after you last night and you were gone so long, I wondered if you were actually having bar bathroom sex."

Anna shuddered. "No. Although, to be totally honest, I would have. I might even have asked him to, but he said to ask him again when I'm sober. He wouldn't even kiss me."

"That man's a keeper."

The words—meant to be funny—struck something deep inside Anna. She knew Finn was a keeper. She wanted to keep him all to herself, but she was trying not to admit that to herself yet. "Anyway, what I need to tell you is not a sexy secret. It's a big, possibly ugly one."

To Eryn's credit, she didn't rush to assure Anna she could keep an ugly secret. She closed her notebook and set it down. "How big are the stakes?"

"My job." She hesitated for a second. "Your job. And possibly worse for another person involved."

"I guess that gives me an idea of who I'll be keeping secrets from. And lying to?"

"I'm hoping it won't come to outright lying, but if it does, I won't expect that." She wasn't really sure yet how far she'd take it if somebody asked *her* straight up about the situation, but she wouldn't ask Eryn to lie for her.

Her assistant narrowed her eyes. "This is about the Bayview Inn, isn't it?"

"I'm not saying anything else until you decide if you want on this ride. If you're not comfortable with it, the conversation ends here with nothing else said. And yeah, you'll wonder what it is and you might even figure it out, but you won't be complicit."

"Fun word, complicit." After a few more seconds of silent deliberation, Eryn stuck out her pinky. "I'm in."

Anna smiled as they locked pinkies. "You didn't even ask if it involves dead bodies."

"When I asked what the stakes were, you didn't mention prison."

"Good point." After taking a deep breath, Anna started talking. She started at the beginning—the very beginning—and wasn't surprised Eryn gasped when she got to the part about her and the electrician sharing a mother.

"I can't believe Brady Nash is your brother. That's wild."

When Anna finally finished talking, Eryn took a moment to digest it all. "Okay, my first question is why you decided to tell me, and why now."

"Because I'm supposed to tell Finn tomorrow if I still want to have sex with him when I'm sober and I do, and there's no way I can keep all these secrets from you. You're going to notice if I'm not here and where am I supposed to tell you I am?"

"But why tell me about the inn? You could tell me you'll be sneaking off with Finn without telling me all the rest."

Anna took a sip of her water and then sighed. "I'm up to my eyeballs in secrets and it's exhausting. It's stressful. And it's hard not having anybody else to talk to about it. I trust you."

"You know I have your back. Always."

She did know that, and tears shimmered in her eyes until she blinked a few times. "I don't want you involved at all. I just don't want you to be blindsided if Duncan finds out about what I'm doing here."

Eryn snorted. "I knew it was something, right from the beginning, but I couldn't figure it out. Now that I know, I'll keep an eye out for anything that could trip you up."

"Thank you." The sense of relief she felt just from talking about it with Eryn made her body feel limp. "Tess built quite the house of cards and I don't want anybody else buried in the rubble if it all comes crashing down."

"There's no reason for that to happen at this point. It probably would have fallen apart in the beginning if it was going to." Eryn rapped her knuckles on the back of the dinette bench, and

Anna chose not to point out it wasn't real wood. She'd settle for any good luck she could get. "Let's go back to the sex. Finn lives with his parents. Where are you planning to have sex with him? Are you going to rent a hotel room for the night?"

She sighed. "Finn made it clear there's no way he and I could rent a room in this town without everybody knowing. And I really want you to be the only person who knows."

"I could go home for the weekend. You'd have the RV to yourself."

"I appreciate the offer, but remember the other night when you sneezed and some woman walking by said 'bless you' and you said 'thank you' and it was so weird? I don't want to have sex with Finn in the RV." She thought about it and then shrugged. "Not the first time, anyway."

Eryn laughed. "Good call."

"I expected you to ask me more questions about the Bayview Inn," Anna said, picking at the label on her water bottle with her thumbnail.

"That never added up to me and there have been questions in the back of my mind since you overturned our decision to put the inn in the rejection pile. I had questions *before*. Now I have answers." Eryn shrugged.

"I'm sorry I put the show at risk, which could affect all of you." Her stomach ached thinking about the possibility of cancellation. "I got wrapped up in the idea that it could be a sign I should find out more about my birth mother. I should have slowed down and thought it through."

"Look at it this way," Eryn replied, holding out her hands. "It's too late to back out now. And I wouldn't even want us to, because Tess is awesome and she deserves our help. But most important, when it comes to the network, this might be the best project we've ever filmed. The Weavers are something else."

Anna laughed, feeling lighter than she had in a while. "That they are."

"And you keep changing the subject back to work." Eryn grinned. "I think the important thing here is that you figure out where you can be alone with Finn."

"I definitely need to give that some thought."

She was still thinking about it when they showed up at Tess's house on Monday morning. And she still didn't have an answer. But he had told her he'd figure something out and he knew Blackberry Bay a lot better than she did, so she'd leave the logistics to him. Assuming he was still interested.

She'd only been on-site for an hour when she got a text message from Finn. Meet me by the storage pods in 5 minutes.

Anna sent back a thumbs-up emoji, but she was

only giving that thumbs-up to meeting him there. She was *not* having sex in a storage pod.

But when she excused herself from a surprisingly heated argument about crown molding, she found him leaned up against one of the pods—one that was out of earshot of the house, but she could see windows and that meant people inside could see her—with his arms folded across his chest.

"It's Monday," he said.

"It hasn't been Monday for very long," she pointed out. "We didn't set a time."

"I couldn't wait anymore," he confessed, and then he gave her a sheepish smile. "Yesterday was a very long day."

"Yeah, so I said some things on Saturday night." She turned her phone over and over in her hands, trying to figure out what to say next.

"Is this where you tell me you were drunk and you didn't mean the things you said?"

That would be the easy—the smart—way out of this, especially since neither his expression nor tone gave any hint of which way he was leaning. She only had his impatience to have this conversation to pin her hopes on. "No. I wasn't as drunk as you think I was and I did mean what I said."

He took a step closer to her, his mouth curving into a smile that—with the help of the heat flaring in his eyes—was somehow a lot naughtier than usual.

Right answer, Anna.

"I know I told you not to forget to kiss me on Monday," she said, jerking her head toward the house. "But maybe not here."

He stopped, but his look told her he hadn't forgotten and that at some point, he was going to catch her alone in a more secluded place. "Okay. I'm going to figure out where we can go on our date, and I'll let you know."

Our date. The way he said it made her smile. "I'll be waiting."

He started walking toward the house, but turned back to wink at her. "You won't be waiting long."

It seemed absolutely ridiculous to Finn that a man of his age and means could not come up with a discreet place to make love to a woman.

It was six o'clock on Monday evening and he was no closer to a solution now than he'd been when he started. And he'd thought about almost nothing else since Saturday night, which made it worse.

The RV was out. Even if Anna got rid of Eryn for a few hours, those things were as soundproof as a window screen. They couldn't go parking because he had his bike and he wasn't even sure he'd fit in her car, never mind get naked in it. Renting a hotel room was out unless they wanted everybody in town to know what they'd been up to by morning.

A tent out in the woods had even crossed his mind. A nice one, with an air mattress and a wicker picnic basket full of wine, crackers and cheese. Lanterns with soft bulbs in them, since candles and tents weren't a great combination. But somehow Anna didn't strike him as the kind of woman who'd happily pee in the woods, so that was out.

He'd take her home to his apartment in Portsmouth—which he felt a really strong desire to do—but she would only end up asking a lot of questions about his life he wasn't sure he could answer. He wanted to focus on her, not on watching every word that came out of his mouth.

Finn had even sent a text message to Brady, asking him if Reyna had rented out the apartment she'd lived in before she moved in with him. She had, of course, just three days before. Renting an apartment just to spend the night with a woman might seem desperate, but he *was* desperate. He was also hoping it would be more than one night.

"Finn, talk some sense into your grandmother," his mother commanded as she walked into the kitchen.

"Can't. I'm working." He waved his hand over the laptop sitting open in front of him on the kitchen table. Luckily, there was a spreadsheet

open to hide the fact he'd done a lot more thinking about the Anna situation than actual work.

"You can work later," Gram said, hot on his
mother's heels. "Somebody has to talk some sense
into your mother."

"When can I work, Gram? In case you forgot,
I spend my days pretending to be a handyman for
your fake inn."

"You can take a break. I read somewhere that
sitting in front of a computer for an entire work-
week takes five years off your life."

"That means I died at least thirty years ago, so
leave me out of this argument, please."

"Tell your grandmother she doesn't need crown
molding."

Finn sighed and saved the spreadsheet so he
could close the laptop. "Gram, you don't need
crown molding."

"Why does your mother hate pretty things,
Finn?"

His mom picked up the dish towel and for a moment he was afraid she was going to flick Gram
with the end of it. But she just twisted it in her
hands. "The expense, Tess. The more Anna spends
on that house, the deeper in trouble you are if she
finds out you lied to her."

"That's a valid point," Finn said, even though
at this point in their deception, what was a little
crown molding going to hurt?

"Anna takes a lot of pride in her work, and she wants her finished homes to look pretty on the show. She's already invested so much that to have her leave something unfinished doesn't seem right."

"If Anna thinks the house needs crown molding, then it needs crown molding," Finn said, pushing back his chair to stand. "If you want to compromise, maybe only the downstairs rooms. I don't know. And I don't care. I'm taking my work up to my room even though my back will hurt tomorrow because ergonomics matter. Good night."

They both muttered a good-night as he picked up the laptop and his notebook and left the kitchen. He usually had a lot more patience when it came to navigating his mother and grandmother's relationship—and certainly more than his dad did—but he wasn't in the mood for it tonight.

The bickering about the amount of money they were getting from *Relic Rehab* made his stomach hurt. He'd spent two days trying to come up with a romantic place to make love to Anna, and they were talking about deceiving her. He understood budgets and advertising and merchandising and he knew they weren't literally taking money out of her pocket. And she was getting the product she was paying for—a beautifully restored historical property.

But it made him uneasy, so when he got to his

room, he actually opened the laptop and made himself focus on work. Maybe later, when his room was dark and he couldn't sleep because his body ached for Anna, the answer would come to him.

Chapter Eleven

"Where are we going?" Anna asked, even though she already knew he was going to tell her it was a surprise.

"It's a surprise." When she opened her mouth to ask another question, he shook his head. "No, you can't get a hint."

She laughed and looked out her window, catching glimpses of the lake through the passing trees. He'd borrowed his dad's truck because there was a chance of rain and while they'd had their first kiss while soaked with cold water, neither of them wanted to see that become a tradition. She'd walked out to the entrance to the campground to meet him, carrying what looked like a beach bag but was doubling as her overnight bag.

Not that she would be gone overnight. When he'd called her and told her he had a plan, but it involved a cancellation and it had to be tonight even though they had to work in the morning, she hadn't even hesitated. She wanted to be with him, even if it was only for a few hours.

Eventually they arrived in another town, though she'd missed the name, and he pulled into the parking lot of a plain-looking motel. "I'll be right back."

By the time he came back with a key and parked in the assigned parking space, she couldn't hold back the laughter anymore.

"Now I know why you wouldn't tell me where we were going," she explained.

"Okay, I know it doesn't look like much, but it's better than a blanket out in the woods. The mosquitoes are rough this time of year."

"I'm just trying to imagine what the desk attendant thinks of me after you said you only need the room for a few hours."

"Confession time. I worked here for a while when I was in high school and I've always kept in touch with the owner. This is a favor for me and I might not have mentioned you. I might have mentioned renovation and Gram and just needing a few hours to get a report finished."

She grabbed her bag and they went up the exterior stairs. She managed to be quiet until he'd closed the door behind them, but then she was laughing again. "A report?"

"I knew I shouldn't have told you that."

Anna grabbed the front of his T-shirt and yanked him toward her. "Actually, I find the lengths you're willing to go to in order to be alone with me very sexy."

"Do you?" He grinned. "I tried to rent an apartment that Reyna owns, but I was a few days too late."

"You didn't." When he nodded, she laughed again. "I don't think I've ever felt so desired in all my life."

"I don't think it's possible for a woman to be desired more than I desire you, Anna. Not without some kind of spontaneous combustion happening." He looked around the room and then back at her. "This isn't a room service kind of place, but I think there's a vending machine if you want anything."

Finn was nervous, she thought. He was worried about making sure everything was okay, when all she wanted was him. She slid her hand over his shoulder and then buried her fingers in his hair. "I'm not here for the snacks."

He kissed her then as if *she* was the snack he'd been craving—devouring her with his mouth until she was panting with need for him. Her body arched against his, yearning for more.

Finally, Finn pulled away just enough to lift her shirt up and over her head and then slid his hands up to cup her breasts. "I've imagined touching you like this every night since I met you."

"And I've imagined being touched by you like this every night."

"It makes it hard to sleep, to be honest."

She laughed. "Worth it, though."

When he pushed down her bra and ran his thumbs over her nipples, she stopped laughing and sucked in a breath. She definitely liked the reality of being touched by him.

She liked it even more when he bent his mouth first to one breast, then the other. Sliding her fingers into his hair, she held him there, wanting more, before deciding to be more proactive.

She managed to get her bra off and her jeans unfastened, but he grabbed her wrist with one hand to stop her from shoving them down. The other hand, he slid over her stomach and under the waistband of her underwear.

He stroked her while she kissed him, until she whimpered and backed away. She appreciated that he wanted to take his time, but she'd been waiting too long for this. "I want you to be naked now."

"We do think alike," he said, grinning. "Because some time in the very near future, I want to take my time getting you out of your clothes. Right now, I just want you to be naked, too."

It was less than a minute before their clothes were in a heap on the floor and, after tossing a wrapped condom on the bedside table, he covered her body with his so he could kiss her some more.

As he kissed her—so deeply and thoroughly she felt it in her soul—they explored each other's bodies with their hands. Touching. Gliding. Grasping. His skin was hot under her fingertips, and she lost herself in the sensations of his hands on her breasts and her stomach and between her thighs until she couldn't take it anymore.

"I want you now," she whispered.

He made a sound against her taut nipple that sounded like agreement, but when he only sucked harder, she gasped. Then she reached out and snagged the wrapped condom.

He chuckled when she slapped it against his chest, but after a short, hard kiss, he took the hint and rolled the condom on. As he settled himself between her thighs, he smiled down at her.

"Have I told you how incredibly beautiful you are?" He ran his thumb over her bottom lip. "Especially your smile. And not your pretty television smile for the cameras. When something makes you happy or you're trying not to laugh, your smile's a little crooked and your eyes crinkle and it lights up your whole face."

"Do *not* make me cry during sex, Finn Weaver," she warned, her voice thick with emotion.

"How about making you cry *out*? Like my name. Can I do that?"

She grinned and scraped her fingernails down his biceps. "You can try."

With a devilish grin that promised his best effort, Finn reached between their bodies and guided himself into her. Her fingertips bit into his back as he slowly pushed and then pulled back until he filled her completely.

She trailed her fingernails over his back, and they bit into his skin as he started thrusting deeply. His gaze locked with hers and she could see what he was feeling in his eyes. Not only heat and pleasure, but happiness. And she felt the same as she buried her fingers in his hair and dragged him down for a hot, messy kiss.

Then he moved faster and she stopped thinking about what he was feeling and lost herself in the pleasure rippling through her body. He watched her, noting what made her gasp, and it wasn't long before the orgasm swept over her. She grasped his shoulders as she came, holding on to him as her body trembled.

He thrust deeper and faster until his muscles tensed under her hands. As his orgasm faded, he lowered himself onto her and his breath was hot and ragged in her hair. She wrapped her arms around him and held him close.

"I'm pretty sure I made you cry out," he whispered when he'd caught his breath.

She chuckled against his neck. "But was it your name?"

"Maybe." He stroked his hand up her side, making her shiver. "You weren't exactly enunciating clearly."

She would have been content to stay the way they were for the rest of the night, but he gently rolled off her. "I'll be right back."

When he disappeared into the bathroom, she rolled onto her stomach and grabbed one of the pillows to support her head. They'd pretty much wrecked the neatly made bed, with the bedspread all crumpled and sideways, and the pillows strewn about. Considering he was supposed to be alone and working, the sight made her chuckle.

"What's so funny?" Finn asked as he slid back onto the bed.

"The owner's going to wonder what kind of report you had to write that involved rolling around on the bed."

He was almost asleep—even though he hadn't intended to nod off since he had to drive them back to town—when Anna asked a question that had him wide awake again in a hurry.

"Where do you disappear to?"

He opened his mouth, but at the last second, he

realized telling her where he actually went could blow up in his face. Or even worse, in Gram's face. Having to think about every single word he said before he said it was the hardest part of this crazy charade. "What do you mean? I took a long lunch break because I had some errands to run."

"And you took yesterday off. You weren't here at all, and that night at The Dock, I hadn't seen you in a week. Tess said you were handling some stuff for your dad, but your dad said you were helping a friend move. Plus, I had walked downtown for a muffin one day and saw you go by on your bike, heading out of town. You seem to randomly disappear."

"It's cute that you think Blackberry Bay actually has a downtown," he said to buy himself a few seconds to think. If he told the truth—that he had business to take care of—she was probably going to wonder what kind of business the handyman for a decrepit fake inn would conduct out of town. Since he was on his Harley, he couldn't even claim he'd gone on a supply run.

"Technically that part of town is a downhill walk from the campground, so it works for me."

"Doesn't it get old, staying in a camper all the time?" It was a pretty slick change of subject, if he did say so himself.

"They're nice campers, we get to see a lot of really pretty parts of New England, and we don't actually spend all that much time in them." She smiled. "So, why don't you want to tell me where you disappear to?"

Maybe not so slick a change of subject, then. He'd assumed she'd be more comfortable talking about herself, but she wasn't going to let it go. Unfortunately, he *had* to lie to her, but maybe he could give her small bits of the truth.

"I help Gram keep up the property." That wasn't a lie at all. He'd been doing odd jobs—including mowing the lawn, trimming hedges and snow blowing—for as long as he could remember. But it lacked enough of the truth to let him look her in the eye as he said it, so he had to give her a little more. "I do have an actual job so I can pay actual bills."

"I figured you either had a job outside of the inn or you stole that Harley."

He laughed with her, even as guilt gnawed at his gut. He hated not being totally honest with her, even if it was for Gram's sake. But maybe he could be a little bit honest with her. In this moment, with her cuddled against his side in bed, it mattered to him.

"When Gram told you I'm the handyman, she meant more of a part-time handyman. I'm her grandson. I've been doing chores for her since I could walk. I think she was afraid you would hold her age against her if you thought she didn't have help and pass over her application, so she might have promoted me from unpaid grandson to unpaid handyman."

"So what do you do when you're not being handy around the house?"

"I'm a financial manager. My business partner and I help people with enough money to need help managing it, but not enough money to have one of the big firms handle it. It's a modest little company, but we do okay."

She pushed herself up to her elbow so she could look down at him. "A financial manager? Really? How have you spent so much time at the house?"

"I sneak away and answer emails and return calls. And I do a lot of work after we're done filming for the day."

Her brow furrowed and he had a moment of fear that he'd blown it. That learning that Gram had claimed her financial manager grandson was the inn's handyman might make her question other things, as well.

"You must be exhausted," she said. "How come your grandmother doesn't have other help? That's a lot to handle alone."

He was going to point out that she'd seen the condition of the house, so maybe handling it alone was a bit of a stretch. But he realized just in time she wasn't talking about Gram handling a large house. She wanted to know how Gram managed a large *inn* by herself.

"She's a pretty stubborn woman," he said, and she dropped her head back as she chuckled. "And it's easy to find cheap, seasonal help in a tourism-driven town."

That wasn't a lie. There were always teenagers looking for temporary jobs during the busy seasons. Not that Gram actually hired any of them, but they were out there.

"We should get dressed," Anna said, sounding sleepy. "If we don't we're going to be doing the walk of shame tomorrow."

"I wish we could stay." He kissed the top of her head. "I like being here with you."

"I like it, too." She stroked her fingertip across his bottom lip. "Maybe next time."

Next time. "You know, anybody who's spent time with my mother and grandmother recently would find it totally believable I'd rent a camper just to get away from them."

She laughed and pushed him toward the edge of the bed, forcing him to get up. "I told you what happened to Eryn and the sneezing. You might not know this about yourself, but you're not very quiet."

"Me?" He scoffed and threw her the bra, which had ended up on top of his pants somehow.

"I happen to have a key to the Bayview Inn,"

she said. "It's closed for renovations, but a thick sleeping bag and a few pillows..."

"That had crossed my mind, but it's my grandmother's house," he said, wrinkling his nose. But he wasn't a man with a lot of options, and Gram technically wasn't living there right now. "I'll think about it."

"I never really understood people who have sex in public places, but we're going to end up in the alley behind the bookstore at the rate we're going."

"I don't think Carly and Zoe would appreciate that," he said, even though he was fairly sure she was joking. When he picked up his phone to slide it into his pocket, he winced. "It's later than I thought."

"I'm almost ready. Tomorrow's going to be a rough day."

He reached out and snagged her hand, pulling her close. "Worth it?"

She lifted onto her toes to kiss him. "So worth it."

Chapter Twelve

"Are you doing anything tonight?" Finn whispered in Anna's ear, and she looked around to make sure nobody was listening. Or looking.

Even if somebody couldn't hear what he was saying, he was a little closer to her than a conversation usually required. When she didn't see anybody, she stepped sideways to close the distance between them.

"What did you have in mind?" It had been three days since their not-quite-overnight trip, and it had been on her mind. A lot. She'd like to do that again sometime soon.

"I was thinking I'd take you for a ride." He paused and then chuckled. "On the bike, I mean."

"Oh." Admiring how he looked on that bike, especially the way his jeans hugged his butt and thighs, was one thing. She hadn't really imagined herself on the back of it, though. "You don't have one of those seats with the big back on it, though."

"No, but it curves up a little to support you. And you can hold on to me." He rested his hand at the small of her back and she shivered. "I won't let you fall off the back, I promise."

"Do you have a helmet for me?"

"Of course. It's my mom's, actually. She used to ride with my dad sometimes, and every once in a while she'll take a ride with me around the lake just to get out."

The idea of going down the road on a motorcycle made her nervous, but she'd watched Finn on it more than she cared to admit. He was comfortable with it and it was obvious he knew what he was doing, and she trusted him to be safe with her on the back.

"That could be fun."

"I promise it will be." The fingers stroking the small of her back dipped just under the waistband of her jeans.

"I'm not having sex with you outside," she said, heading that off at the pass. "Or on your motorcycle, because that doesn't look fun no matter what *Playboy* magazine says."

"We can kiss, though, right?" She nodded because that wasn't even a question. She always wanted to kiss him. "Should I pick you up at the RV about seven?"

"I'll meet you at the entrance to the campground at seven." She'd tell Eryn where she was going, of course, but if she played her cards right, the rest of the crew would never know she left her RV. Fewer questions that way.

When the day finally ended—later than it should have due to somebody not being great with a measuring tape—she was tired, but she jumped in the shower and made herself a chicken salad sandwich for dinner.

"You're running out on me again?" Eryn asked from her usual spot on the tiny couch. "Where to tonight?"

"He's taking me for a ride on the bike." She wasn't sure which of the butterflies in her stomach were nervousness and which were excitement, but they were all fluttering in there together.

"You're going to want to take that ponytail out and either do a low pony at the base of your neck or braid it. The lump under your helmet might give you a headache after a while." When Anna looked at her with surprise, because nothing about her assistant screamed *biker chick*, Eryn shrugged. "I dated a girl in college who had a beat-up motorcycle. We had a blast with that thing. I think I liked the bike more than I liked her, actually. When we broke up, I really missed it."

Laughing, Anna went back into the bathroom and redid her hair so it was pulled back below where her helmet would sit. Then, after putting her license and a credit card in her back pocket, she grabbed her phone and said goodbye to Eryn.

It was a short walk to the campground entrance, which was around a wooded corner, so it was out of sight of the RVs. She heard the rumble of the Harley's engine before he came into sight, and as he pulled up beside her, the nervous butterflies kicked into high gear.

After he'd turned it off and leaned it onto the kickstand, Finn swung his leg over the bike and pulled her in for a long kiss.

"You're shaking," he said. "We don't have to do this if you're not sure."

"I want to. I'm nervous about it, but that doesn't mean I don't want to try it."

"If you want to stop, just tap me on the shoulder and I'll find a place to pull over. And if you want to come back, tell me. I don't care if we've gone five hundred feet or five miles, okay?"

Reassured she could trust Finn to take care of her, she nodded and accepted the helmet and sunglasses he handed her. He had to help her with the buckle, and then he pulled a lightweight leather jacket out of one of his side bags.

"This is Mom's, too. It'll be a little big on you, but as the sun starts going down, it can get chilly. And it's just good protection." He laughed at her expression. "You ever been hit by a June bug on bare skin at sixty miles an hour? Trust me."

It took her two tries to get on the bike behind him. The first time, she panicked when the bike dipped slightly, but he assured her he had it balanced and they wouldn't fall over. And he only laughed at her a little bit. The second time, she was able to get her leg up and over so she could straddle the seat behind him. It was comfortably cushioned and slightly higher than his seat, so she could see over his shoulder.

She wasn't sure if that was a good thing or a bad thing.

When she put her hands tentatively at his waist, he turned and spoke with a raised voice so she could hear him through the helmet. "You can hold on however you want. This is fine, or you can wrap your arms around me if you want. And if you get nervous in a corner, don't try to sit up straight. Just relax against my back and you'll naturally lean with me. Okay?"

She nodded, but when he fired up the engine and the massive bike vibrated through her body, she leaned against him and wrapped her arms around his stomach. He patted her hand, and then, with a rev of the engine, they were moving.

It was both terrifying and exhilarating at first, but it didn't take long for her to relax and enjoy the novelty of having nothing between her and the gorgeous landscape they were passing through. With the lake on one side and either woods or gorgeous waterfront homes on the other, she spent most of the ride looking from one side to the other. She was barely aware of the fact her hands were resting lightly on his hips, though she relaxed against his back whenever there was a corner coming.

Anna wasn't sure how far from Blackberry Bay they were when he slowed and turned onto a dirt road. The bike felt different, almost squirrelly, and even though Finn didn't seem too concerned about it, she wrapped her arms around his midsection again.

When they broke into a clearing on the banks of a river, she decided the dirt road had been worth it. He pulled to a stop and put his feet down to balance the bike, and then he tapped her leg and motioned for her to get off. She managed to do it without pulling a muscle or falling off, and then unbuckled her helmet while he walked the bike backward to turn it around. After parking it, he took his helmet off and set it on the seat. He put hers with it, and then gave her a questioning look.

"What do you think?"

"I can see why you spend so much time on it.

I'm enjoying myself, except for the dirt road part. I'm not sure I like that."

"I could tell that from the Heimlich you gave me when we first left the pavement," he teased, and then he took her hand.

They walked along the riverbank, hand in hand, and Anna felt more at peace than she had for a very long time. "It's beautiful here."

"This has always been one of my favorite spots. My dad and I used to fish here sometimes. Mostly I played on the rocks, though."

"I haven't done that in so many years," she said wistfully, looking at all the rocks sticking up out of the river.

He let go of her hand and gestured toward the river. "Now's your chance."

"Isn't that something kids do?"

"Why? Was there an age cutoff I missed for doing things that make us happy?"

"You're right." She reached up and cupped his face so she could bring him in for a kiss. A long, slow kiss on a riverbank on a warm summer night. "That makes me happy."

And then she turned and stepped out onto a large flat rock. She moved from rock to rock, choosing each one carefully and testing it first as she moved further out into the river. When one shifted under her foot, she squealed and jumped back, and then she turned when she heard Finn's laughter right behind her.

"You didn't think I'd let you have all the fun without me, did you?" he asked. "But maybe not that rock."

She laughed and turned back to scout out her next rock, wondering if she could make it all the way to the other side of the river and back without getting wet.

"I think you're keeping secrets from me, Anna Beckett."

He said the words in a light—almost teasing— tone, but some of the color seemed to drain from her face as her eyes widened. He probably shouldn't have brought it up while they were balancing on rocks in the middle of a river.

"What do you mean?"

"I heard an interesting rumor today," he said, suddenly concerned that he'd opened a can of worms he couldn't put the lid back on, and she didn't look happy about it.

"Oh, really?" She stepped onto another rock, maybe to give herself something to look at besides him.

"According to the grapevine, you're the daughter nobody in Blackberry Bay knew Christy Nash had."

He could tell by the way her body stiffened that he'd hit a nerve.

"That is an interesting rumor," she said while neither confirming nor denying it. The way she drew out the words gave him the impression she was trying to buy herself time to think.

"Kind of a coincidence you'd end up in this town."

"Did Brady say something to you?"

"So Brady knows?" He'd been hoping his best friend hadn't been keeping something this big from him, but it was obvious she and Brady had talked, and she nodded the confirmation.

Anna was Brady's half sister. That was something it would take him a while to wrap his mind around.

On the heels of that thought came another. Did Brady know he and Anna were seeing each other? He'd thought their night in the motel was their secret, but obviously there were conversations happening he wasn't a part of.

"I knew my birth mother was from this area, but I didn't know she was still here. I was born in Colorado, so I just assumed she was still there." She picked what had to have been a very tiny piece of lint off her sleeve, since he couldn't see it. "Of course I recognized the name of the town when the team reviewed your grandmother's application, and I was looking forward to seeing some of the places where my mom would have been when she was a kid. I didn't expect to actually meet her."

"That's quite a coincidence," he said, and then he wanted to kick himself. Gram's application was *not* something he wanted anybody dwelling on, but especially not Anna. He decided it was best to steer Anna away from how she'd ended up here and more toward her family. "You've actually met Christy, then?"

"Brady drove me to her house and we talked. Not for long, but enough to break the ice, I guess."

Finn remembered the day Brady had gone to Gram's house to go over the electrical with the *Relic Rehab* crew—the way he'd stopped short and stared at Anna. He supposed there was a resemblance between mother and daughter, though he hadn't really noticed it until he'd heard somebody whispering about it at the café.

"Who told you?" she asked, squinting at him because the sun was low behind him and probably reflecting off the river.

"I'm actually not sure who was doing the talking, but I heard two women whispering about it when I stopped at the café to grab a breakfast sandwich. It was just speculation, but it rang true. So I guess you and everybody else involved should know it's not really a secret anymore."

"I'm probably the only person who cared if it was a secret, but I'm a pretty private person. My husband cheating with a professional rival of mine and our subsequent divorce was well covered by the tabloids, so I'm not one for sharing a lot these days."

He knew she'd been divorced. He wasn't sure if she'd mentioned it in passing or if one of his family members had talked about it. But this was the first time he heard the lingering hurt and bitterness in her voice, and he could see why she wouldn't want her personal life on display, even in as benign a way as small-town gossip.

"Obviously you and Brady are doing okay," he said, trying to ignore his annoyance with his best friend for not telling him what was going on. It was probably a tough spot for Brady to be in. "How did your meeting with Christy go?"

"Better than I expected, actually." Her face softened, and he wished they weren't standing on rocks in the river, so he could wrap his arms around her. "I thought I would have a lot more anger, but it turns out that she really did just do what was best for me, out of love. It's hard to fault her for that. My dad? I'm still struggling with him a little because keeping it a secret made it much more traumatic for me than it needed to be."

Secrets definitely made a mess of things, and that awareness made him uncomfortable. He hated that he was keeping secrets from Anna, and it made him sad to imagine how different things could be if he wasn't hiding things from her and they could live their lives on their own terms.

"So you'll have a relationship with Christy, then?" he asked. Maybe the town grapevine buzzing about her wouldn't be as painful if there was no reason to keep it a secret.

"Yes, I think so. I'm actually having dinner with the entire family tomorrow night. I guess they usually do it on Fridays, but I haven't met Chris yet and they're going on vacation, so…tomorrow it is. Since you already know about me and Christy, and you're practically part of their family anyway, do you want to come with me?"

"It seems like kind of a big deal for you," he said. "With a lot of people. Are you looking for an ally?"

"Not an ally, really." She gave a nervous little laugh. "I'd say it's more like taking you home to meet my family, but you've known my family your entire life and I'm the one meeting some of them, so…"

Like a boyfriend. The thought brought a rush of pleasure, and he hopped to a rock that was closer to her so he could take her hand. Then he lifted it to his mouth and kissed her palm.

"I would be honored to go with you to your family dinner."

She giggled in a way that made him feel young again, and he held her hand as they navigated the rocks back to shore. Then he kissed her softly, his hands on her waist.

"This has been a very good day," she whispered against his lips.

"It's not over yet," he whispered back before he kissed her some more.

She was right. Today had been a very good day—one of the best, except for the little black rain cloud always hovering in the back of his mind to remind him that all of this was fleeting.

Even if she never found out the truth about the Bayview Inn, he knew. It ate at him every time he was with her and if not for the possible repercussions Gram could face, he would have confessed long ago. But he couldn't.

And whether she found out the truth or not, she wasn't staying in Blackberry Bay. She had a home in Connecticut. A successful television show. Book tours and whatever else she had going on in her life. One way or another, he was going to have to let her go eventually.

Just not today.

Chapter Thirteen

They had reached the part of the renovation where the time flew by, and Anna was exhausted by the end of each day. They all were, but it was also the part of the renovation where it all started coming back together. This week they'd begun the process of refinishing the hardwood floors, as well, now that the heavier construction was over.

And a lot of work was getting done in the kitchen, too. Brady had been in and out over the course of the week, doing electrical as needed, and they'd be putting the new cabinets in soon. Anna liked to refinish original cabinetry as much as possible, but the Bayview Inn's kitchen was so out of date that the large and clunky wood had to go.

She'd just gotten off the phone with the company delivering the counter and vanity tops when Tess walked into the kitchen. She was bent over slightly, one hand pressed to her back, and Anna was thankful Tess had accepted the suggestion that her bedroom be moved downstairs. It had upped the budget more than she liked, but it was worth it to make sure Tess's home worked for her as well as future guests.

Assuming the Bayview Inn ever actually became an inn. Anna had her doubts about that. Not only because Tess's family had their own lives to return to and it would be too much for her to handle alone. But also because she couldn't imagine the older woman having the patience or tact to host strangers in her home. She adored Tess, but she was a handful.

"You look tired today," Anna said gently. "You know you don't have to be here, right? We can work around you for the day. And Alice and Joel are learning how to miter trim board corners. That'll give Mike and Cody plenty of filming opportunities."

Tess waved her hand as if didn't matter. "I'm fine. Just feeling a little overwhelmed today. It's a lot of change for an old bird like me."

"I know, but I think you'll find it's all worth it in the end, and with a fresh new inside, this grand old house will be easier to keep up."

"It's a lot," Tess said in an uncharacteristically quiet voice. "This grand old house is definitely a lot to take care of, and the older she and I get, the more run-down we look and feel."

It broke Anna's heart to hear the thread of despair woven through the older woman's words, but she knew she had to choose her words carefully. She didn't want to let on that she knew about Tess's scheme to get help, and she was also afraid that in her current mood, the older woman might say something that would incriminate her.

"Once the work is done and you can move back in, she'll feel like home again. You'll feel better when we're all gone."

Tess frowned and shook her head. "I don't know about that. I like having you around. Maybe not the cameras and the other folks, but I wouldn't mind if you stayed."

You are not going to cry right now, Anna told herself firmly. "I like it here, too."

She liked Blackberry Bay and Tess and Brady and all of them a lot, but she didn't want her mind latching on to the idea of staying. The problem was that she liked Finn most of all, and she couldn't help wondering how she would feel if *he* was talking about her staying and not his grandmother.

Her watch vibrated and she checked the notification to find a text message from Finn. Are you almost done?

Even though she'd already met and spent time with Brady and Christy, she'd woken up incredibly anxious about tonight's dinner. That was a lot of family she didn't know under one roof.

But she shouldn't have worried. Chris was as wonderful as Brady. Not quite as outgoing, maybe, but kind and interested without being nosy. His wife, Marcy, was a teacher, and their boys, CJ and Benny, were a handful. Wrapping her mind around suddenly being an aunt to three nephews was a lot to process, but in a good way. And she'd already put their birthdates in her calendar so she could send gifts when the time came.

She already knew Reyna fairly well thanks to the new cupcake addiction she and Eryn had acquired. Once it was known Anna and Reyna were actually sisters-in-law, the length of time they spent chatting in the bakery had increased, and she liked Brady's wife a lot. She hoped to find time to have lunch or a girls' night with her before they wrapped up filming.

The dinner was actually a barbecue, so overall, it was a casual evening of them getting to know each other. Watching Finn with CJ, Benny and Parker was her favorite part, though. He had a way with the boys, and they all clearly adored him. They were comfortable together, and eventually Anna found herself sitting on the floor with them, building tall structures out of blocks that the boys could knock down. Judging by their laughter, it was a favorite activity of theirs.

"They like you," he said quietly when the boys were lured away for a few minutes by the offering of pudding cups.

"They're adorable. So much energy, though."

"Do you see yourself having kids someday?" He asked the question casually enough, but she got the impression by the way he looked at her that he cared about her answer.

"I think so." She sighed and looked at the boys who were feeding themselves pudding with varying degrees of success. Vanilla was definitely the right choice. "I was pretty focused on my career during my short marriage, and after the divorce… well, there was a lot more focus on my career. But I don't see myself *not* having kids someday. What about you?"

"Yeah. I definitely want kids. I always assumed I would in a vague, someday sort of way, but since Parker came along and I've watched Brady with him, it's not really a question anymore. I definitely want children, when the time is right."

"Somebody needs to have a girl," she said, and they both laughed.

They were interrupted, then, by Marcy and Christy wanting to know more about how filming was going and what it was like to be on TV, but throughout the rest of the evening, Anna's gaze was constantly drawn to Finn and the kids.

This, she thought, looking around the large, loud and obviously happy family group. This was definitely something she wanted in her future. And it was Finn's face she saw when she imagined who would be at her side.

She wanted to build a life—a family—like this with him. And even though the thought made her smile, deep down it scared the crap out of her. Sneaking around for motorcycle rides and amazing sex was one thing.

Putting her heart out there was another thing entirely.

The next day was a light day for the family because the crew was filming Anna doing something they called walk-throughs, which appeared to mean she walked through the rooms and talked about what they'd done so far and what they hoped to accomplish next. It involved a lot of talking and a lot of takes, so when his mother showed up with Grizz, Finn took advantage of the fact nobody cared what he was doing and went outside to play with the dog.

"Oh good, you're here," his mom said. "Can you watch him for a little while? I want to talk to your dad about a few things and I don't want to bring him in with me."

"I'm always up for dog-sitting."

They played fetch for a while, using the raggedy old ball Grizz always brought with him for car trips. He loved riding in the car and it usually meant seeing new people. Those people didn't always have balls or sticks to throw, so he brought his own.

But it was a warm day, so eventually they sat in the shade of a big elm tree and Finn idly rubbed the dog's head. When he saw Anna step onto the front porch, her gaze scanning the yard, he waved to her.

As she walked over, he kept one finger under Grizz's collar to hold him still. He wanted to see Anna and if she got distracted by a dog running to meet her, she might not make it as far as his shady spot.

"Time for a break," she said, sitting in the grass next to him. He released the dog's collar, and he immediately leaped into Anna's lap. "Who is this?"

"This is Grizz, the grizzly bear. He's my dog."

Anna looked up at him. "Wait, you have a dog?"

"Okay, fine," he said. "He's my parents' dog, which means he's the family dog and I'm part of the family, so he's kind of mine."

She laughed and scratched under Grizz's chin, which meant his dog would now love Anna forever. "That's a big, fierce name for a little peanut of a dog."

"He might be little, but he's always believed in his heart that he's actually a grizzly bear and behaves accordingly."

"That's a very good way to go through life," she said in a higher-pitched way that made Grizz immediately roll onto his back so she could rub his belly. He writhed in ecstasy while Finn rolled his eyes.

"You're officially his best friend forever now," he said.

"I bet Grizz has a lot of best friends."

She was right. "He's a pretty friendly guy overall. But if for whatever reason he doesn't like somebody, he can be a little ferocious about it."

"I never got to have a pet growing up because my...my mom is allergic to everything."

Finn caught the slight pause before she said *mom*, but he didn't comment on that. He assumed she meant her stepmother, and once again he was struck by how difficult that must have been for a teenage girl. "I can't imagine not having a dog in my life. Leaving Grizz every time I come visit never gets any easier."

"You don't have a dog of your own?"

"I don't live in a dog-friendly place. They need room to run and play, and I'd feel guilty about a dog being alone while I'm working. Tom wouldn't care if we had a dog in the office, but we have a

lot of meetings and, believe it or not, not everybody likes dogs."

"True, but do you really want to be doing business with people who don't like dogs?"

He laughed with her. "No, I don't."

"I'd like to see your apartment," she said in a
rather abrupt change of subject.

"It's not very exciting."

She laughed. "Maybe not, but I'm curious what
your life is like when you're not helping Tess
around the inn."

"I wouldn't mind taking you there." Maybe it
would be a little risky to give her that much of a
glimpse into his life, but it wasn't as if she didn't
already know he wasn't *only* the inn's handyman.
The problem was having her figure out he wasn't
really the handyman at all and going digging to
see what else wasn't true.

But he wanted to take her home with him. He
wanted to take her out for a nice dinner and then
make love to her in his own bed. And he very
much wanted to fall asleep with her in his arms
and wake up next to her.

"Do you have any plans this weekend?" she
asked as she tossed the ragged ball for Grizz to
fetch.

He'd planned to hole up in his room with his
laptop, but it definitely wouldn't take much to

change his mind. "Nothing much. Do you have something in mind?"

Grizz seemed to have given up on the game, choosing instead to watch some birds flitting around the gardens, so Anna drew her knees up and wrapped her arms around her legs.

"I bet I could talk Eryn into going home for the weekend. She misses her wife and their kiddo when we're on location, and it's a long drive, but she's used to it," she said. Even though she was watching Grizz, he could see the tinge of pink on her cheeks. "I could tell the crew she and I are making the trip back together, but then she could drop me off with you and I'd be off the grid for the weekend."

"How clandestine," he said, and her cheeks darkened. "I like it."

"I'll try to wrap up a little early on Friday, because it's a five-hour drive for Eryn. Then she'll have to pick me up somewhere in town on her way back Sunday evening, since I was supposed to be with her and they'll notice if she returns without me."

"She knows, then? That you'll be with me?"

"I know I said I didn't want anybody to know, but it's hard to keep secrets from a woman who is not only my assistant, but my RV roommate."

"If she's on board, then we'll go. It would be nice to go away with you."

Neither of them heard his mother coming across the lawn until she was almost upon them and Grizz jumped up to greet her as if she'd been gone a week. "I was wondering where you got off to. And Grizz, of course. He can go from sleeping to up to his ears in trouble in the blink of an eye."

"We played some ball," Anna told her. "Now he's stalking the birds. I'm pretty sure they're taunting him, actually."

"I'm sure he deserves it." She looked at Finn, and her gaze was full of questions and speculation. He hadn't realized how close he and Anna were sitting until just that second. They weren't touching, but they were definitely in each other's personal space.

Finn sat up straight so he wasn't leaning toward Anna anymore, but judging by the quirk of his mother's eyebrow, it didn't really help.

Then Anna pushed herself to her feet and tapped at something on her watch. "I would rather sit here and watch Grizz play for the rest of the day, but I should get back inside."

"Finn's going to help me get Grizz in the car so I can take him home," Alice said, "but then he'll be along."

That was definitely a maternal signal that he was about to get a talking-to, but Finn stood up and very deliberately did *not* watch Anna walk back to the house. Instead he started toward the dog, who wasn't going to be happy to leave his new favorite game of running in circles while yipping at birds.

He wasn't surprised when his mother followed him, or when she put her hand on his arm before he could bend over and pick up Grizz.

"Have you totally lost your mind, child?" she demanded.

He was tempted to point out he was far from being a child, but he knew better. "What do you mean?"

"Don't play coy with me. You two have had your eyes on each other since day one, but I didn't think you were actually foolish enough to get involved with the woman your grandmother has us actively defrauding every single day that she's here."

He wanted to deny it, or at least skirt around the truth, but he didn't bother. One, she already knew. Motherly instincts and all that. And two, he didn't want to lie to his mother. It gave him a stomachache and never ended well.

"One thing has nothing to do with the other," he said, which wasn't an outright admission of guilt.

"Finn." Her sigh had just enough of a growl in it to make him wince.

"I would *never* throw Gram under the bus, Mom. Not for anything or anybody. You know that."

"I do know that. But it's easy to slip up and

make a stupid mistake, and it's even easier to slip up if you're spending time together alone. It's a lot of risk for a fling."

A fling? Something about the words made him want to instantly reject them—to tell her he wasn't sure it was just a fling. But he didn't. "I'm well aware of the stakes, and this isn't something you need to worry about."

"I hope not." She bent over and picked up Grizz, giving lie to the notion she'd needed help in the first place. "If you can't keep your fly shut, make sure you keep your mouth shut."

"Mom!" He shook his head and took a step toward the house. "I'm done talking about this. I love you and I'll see you when I get home."

"Love you, too, honey."

What a mess, he thought as he walked up the porch steps. Not that his mother was wrong, exactly. But he didn't want to talk to her about intimate details of his personal life, *ever.*

And he didn't want to give up Anna.

Chapter Fourteen

"This isn't what I expected," Anna said, turning in a circle in the middle of Finn's apartment.

"I'm almost afraid to ask what you thought my home would look like," he said, tossing his keys and wallet on the table next to the door.

"I don't know. Like a bachelor pad or more... plain, maybe? This room looks like it could be a room in your grandmother's house." When he nodded and gave her a sheepish grin, she got it. "That's why you picked it, isn't it? The older building, with an outdated apartment. It reminds you of home."

"That and the garage space for my bike."

"You do have a lot less stuff than Tess, which is good."

"And most of it was made in the last decade."

Despite the teasing, his place *did* have a similar vibe as his grandmother's house. It was in the structure of the apartment and the possibly original wooden floors and trim. It didn't have the sleek updated look so many apartments had, but kept the original charm of the historic building it was in. His furniture was leather, but worn and soft, and there were a lot of small touches she hadn't expected. An old quilt on the back of the couch. Place mats on the wooden table. A few houseplants that were probably in desperate need of water.

"Are you going to give me the grand tour?" she asked, trailing her fingertips down his arm.

"I don't know about grand. It's not a big place."

She laughed and took his hand in hers. "I'm just trying to get in your bedroom, Finn."

"Oh." He chuckled and pulled her toward the door on the other side of the living room. "Definitely a grand tour, then."

The bedroom was decorated with the same type of comfortable, homey furniture as the rest of the apartment. A solid maple dresser and matching nightstands. A sturdy chair with a lamp tucked to the side as though that was where he did his reading. And an old-fashioned brass bed covered by a soft down comforter she couldn't wait to mess up.

Once Finn put his hands on her, she stopped admiring his decor, except for the brass headboard. The rails were perfect for holding on to as he kissed his way down her body—pausing to lavish attention on her breasts and then nipping at the inside of her thighs before he settled his mouth against her.

He licked and sucked until she cried out and her back arched off the bed. Only when she'd had the first of what she hoped would be many orgasms this weekend did he pull a condom from the drawer and roll it on.

Finn took his time making love to her, kissing her and stroking her hair away from her face as he thrust slowly into her. When she cupped the side of his face in one hand, and he turned to kiss her palm, she felt her heart squeeze in her chest.

Her heart, she thought as she ran her finger over his lip. It wasn't just her body being thrilled by being in Finn's bed. Her heart was involved and when she looked into his eyes and saw the emotion there, she knew it was too late to do a damn thing about it.

Then he drew her finger into his mouth and sucked hard as he thrust deeper into her and all of her attention went back to the delicious sense of friction and heat.

It wasn't until much later, when they lay breathless and depleted in each other's arms that she let herself think about the connection they had. It wasn't just physical. She couldn't deny her feelings, and she also couldn't deny what she saw in his eyes when he looked at her.

She loved him. And she was growing ever more certain that he loved her.

No matter how hard she tried—wanting to savor the possibilities between them—she couldn't push back the reality. They were still lying to each other. And maybe they'd wrap filming and the show would air and nobody would ever be the wiser.

But they'd know. And she couldn't shake the fear that having the Bayview Inn secret between them, even if it never blew up in their faces, would be like having a tiny stone in your shoe. You could keep walking, but eventually it was going to hurt.

"What are you thinking about?" he murmured into her hair.

"I'm not really thinking about anything," she said, closing her eyes against yet another lie.

"That was a pretty big sigh for a woman who's not thinking about anything."

"Fine. I was wondering what the chances are I can steal this bed without you noticing. I *really* like this bed."

He chuckled and squeezed her tight. "I'd probably notice if you tried to steal it, but feel free to spend the entire weekend in it with me."

But they needed food to keep their strength up, so on Saturday, they explored the city. He took her to his favorite breakfast café, and then they walked around the historical districts. In the afternoon, they took the bike and rode along the coast, stopping at a few of the beaches and historical spots. She could see that he liked Portsmouth, but he didn't light up the way he did when he talked about Blackberry Bay. He might not even realize it, but most of the things he'd made a point to share with her reminded her of his hometown.

They ate fresh seafood at a place that didn't look like much, but he'd only told her to trust him and he hadn't let her down yet. They made love again, and on Sunday morning, her first waking thought was regret that the weekend was over.

"I wish we didn't have to go back," he said sleepily, as if he'd read her mind, and kissed her hair. "Not yet at least."

She closed her eyes, surprised by the emotion that welled up inside of her. She didn't want to go back, either. "If we don't go back, the inn won't get finished and Tess will have to live with your parents indefinitely."

"I think you just threatened me with my father showing up at my door and dragging us both home."

Home. That was how he thought of Blackberry Bay, and he probably always would. But it wasn't her home. Her life wasn't there, and every day she worked on the Bayview Inn was another day closer to her having to make a choice.

A few weeks ago, she would have said there was no choice. Her home was in Connecticut, as was her career and her sisters. But now she wasn't so sure, because when she thought of home, she thought of Finn.

Determined to put off their return until the last possible minute, Anna rolled to face him and ran her fingernails down his chest. "We still have a few hours before we have to leave."

"Breakfast is overrated anyway."

"So is talking," she said, and then she silenced him with a kiss.

"I like working on this house a lot more when there aren't cameras in my face," Finn said, looking at the electrical panel Brady had his hands in.

"Probably because you're actually standing around talking and not actually working," Brady replied. "And even though you haven't done anything, you're still a better fake electrician than you are a fake plumber."

"You heard about that, huh?"

"One of the cool perks of Anna turning out to be my sister is that I get to hear things about you that you would never tell me."

Finn shrugged. "I would have told you, eventually. Dad probably would have beat me to it, though. I don't think I've seen him laugh that hard in years."

"I'll set my DVR to record that episode."

They were not only alone in Gram's house, but they were working in the cool cellar updating the electrical lines running from the kitchen. To fit it into Brady's schedule and be at a time when Reyna would be home with Parker, the two of them had come back after everybody else left, and it felt like the most peace and quiet Finn had had in ages. He would rather have spent the time with Anna, but a guys' night out with Brady—even if it was in Gram's cellar and involved working—was the next best thing.

It would be better if they were kicked back drinking a couple of beers, but he supposed drinking and wiring was frowned upon, as it should be.

"So I've got some gossip for you," Brady said, and then he picked up a coil of wire and held it out. "Here, hold this."

"What kind of gossip?"

"Reyna had lunch with Sydney and Meredith today and Sydney told her the word around town is that you and Anna are seeing each other."

"I knew that already."

Brady shot him a look that should have melted the wire he was holding. "But did you know people are talking about it?"

"I think it was probably inevitable in this town. And we're kind of trying to keep it quiet, but we're seen together. I've taken her out on the bike a couple of times. We had breakfast at the café. I don't think it's really a problem."

"Except the people being asked to go along with the Bayview Inn nonsense are the same people who know you're seeing the star of *Relic Rehab*. You've got so many grapes on the grapevine that people are going to start jumping up and down and making wine."

"I don't think it's quite that scandalous. I mean, look at her. It would be more newsworthy if I *wasn't* attracted to her."

"Hey, that's my sister you're talking about." Brady frowned when Finn gave him a questioning look, and then he shrugged. "I'm pretty sure I'm supposed to say that."

"You've known her like five minutes," Finn said.

"Doesn't make her not my sister."

"True."

Brady sighed. "This is weird, on so many different levels."

"Trust me, I know. I finally find a woman like Anna and then—*surprise*—she's my best friend's secret sister."

"Since we're on the subject, what exactly are your intentions?"

Finn laughed at first, but he stopped when he realized Brady wasn't laughing with him. He hadn't even cracked a smile. "Wait, are you serious? It's not 1890 anymore, you know."

"I know, but you have this look. Like… I don't know. I think you're falling for her pretty hard and I'd be happy for you if I didn't know you've been lying to her." He took a swig of beer and then shook his head. "This seems like a good time to point out that I haven't had to lie to my sister, but I've had to *not* tell her the truth, and there is no aspect of your life right now that isn't giving me a headache."

"Tell me about it."

"I want you to tell me the truth of what's going on between you."

"I can't speak for her, but…" He fiddled with the end of the wire in his hands. "It's serious for me."

"I'm glad for you because I really want you to have what I have. It's pretty amazing, Finn. But at some point you're going to have honesty in your relationship or it's going to go south on you."

"You know that's the one thing I can't do. Not with everything Gram has at stake," Finn said, and he really did not want to talk about this anymore tonight. "Why am I still holding this wire?"

"Because I told you to."

"What's it for, though?"

Brady sighed. "Because it was starting to piss me off that you were standing around doing nothing, so now you're doing something. You're hold-ing that wire."

When Finn chucked it at his head, Brady ducked and his laugh echoed around the old stone walls of the foundation.

"I was wrong. You're an even worse fake elec-trician than you are a fake plumber."

When they finally called it a night and Brady dropped him off in front of his parents' house, he looked at his watch, but it was too late to call Anna. Maybe he could send her a text message because that was less intrusive, but he wanted to hear her voice.

And maybe it was pointless anyway. He wanted to have a conversation with her—a *real* conversation—and find out where she saw their relationship going. He was already in over his head, so if she wasn't on the same page, the sooner he got out, the less it would hurt.

But how could he have that conversation with her and maybe even talk about a future together when he couldn't be honest with her?

When he saw Grizz staring at him from the back of the couch, which enabled him to see out the window, Finn gave up on talking to Anna to-night and went inside. He knew he needed to say something to Anna soon—he needed her to know he was all in on their relationship. But he wasn't sure what that meant yet other than the sense of urgency he felt for the remodeling to be done so he could put Gram's latest escapade behind him had changed into dreading that final day, because it meant Anna would be leaving.

He didn't want her to go.

That was the one concrete thing he knew. He couldn't imagine not having Anna in his life anymore, and he didn't want to. But he hadn't figured out the hard parts. They couldn't just...stay together in Blackberry Bay, with neither of them leaving. He had a home and a business in Portsmouth. Her home was in Connecticut and she had the show.

And then there was the biggest hurdle of all—one he couldn't see any way over. If she stayed, the truth about the Bayside Inn was going to come out. Maybe she'd just find out in town one day when people got tired of playing Tess Weaver's game and it slipped out. He liked to think he'd tell her himself because it was the right thing to do, but the fear she'd walk away made his stomach hurt.

He couldn't see how they'd get past the lies he and his family had told her.

When Grizz whined for his attention, maybe sensing Finn's mood, he sat on the couch and patted his lap. If there was one thing Finn *did* know, it was that rubbing a dog's belly always made a person feel better.

Chapter Fifteen

"Is the crew here yet?" Anna asked Eryn after looking out the front window for what felt like the tenth time.

"No. Do you want me to call Mike?"

"Let's give them ten more minutes." It was odd, though. Sometimes they came in a little later if they'd worked into the night, to make up time, but they usually let Eryn know. They were also aware there was a lot on their plate today, since Eryn had sent Mike the list of scenes Anna had dictated.

Anna and Eryn had left earlier than usual that morning so they could stop at the café and have an actual sit-down breakfast, rather than something on the run, so they hadn't seen any of the crew before they left the campground.

When Anna's watch notified her she had a call, she thought it might be one of the guys and pulled her phone out of her pocket. But Duncan Forrest's name was on the screen and she hesitated, actually considering sending him to voice mail. Not only was it rare for them to call this early in the day, but a call from Duncan directly to Anna was usually scheduled in advance. Otherwise, Eryn communicated with their assistants.

But she knew if she put off the call, she'd only obsess about it, so she answered it as she went down the hall and out the front door to find a quiet place to talk. "Hello?"

"Anna, it's Duncan." He still didn't seem to understand how caller ID worked on cell phones. "I received a rather disturbing call from Mike yesterday. Apparently, neither you nor Eryn answered your phones, so he decided to loop me in."

She froze, one foot on the bottom porch step and one foot on the walkway. "Disturbing how?"

"As I understand it, the young cameraman—Cody, I believe his name is—was out on the town and spent some time with a young local woman. She told him quite the tale about the Bayview Inn."

Even though she was standing in bright morning sunshine, Anna shivered. She felt compelled to move further from the house in question, and she ended up leaning against their car.

Maybe she could save it. If the local woman had been drinking and Cody had been drinking, and then it passed through Mike, she couldn't be sure what Duncan actually knew.

"Do you care to share the tale she told?"

"That Tess Weaver falsified documents to apply to *Relic Rehab* and has coerced the residents of the town into corroborating her story."

Well, he knew everything he needed to know, then. She needed to be very, very careful about what she said next. No matter what he said, she wanted to neither confirm nor deny. But he didn't even give her a chance to respond.

"We're not really sure how you let this happen, Anna. We were able to confirm the history of the Bayview Inn is nothing but a fiction created by the Weaver family with just a cursory examination."

The censure in his tone grated over her nerves like sandpaper, but the underlying fear for Tess was stronger than her fear of being admonished by disappointed bosses.

"So maybe Tess Weaver exaggerated the Bayview Inn's historical significance," Anna admitted, since she didn't really have a choice. The Bayview Inn wasn't even an inn. "But you've seen at least some of the footage. Our audience isn't going to care about some fudging of the building's history, because the Weavers are one of the most entertaining families we've ever had on the show. I think it'll have the highest ratings of any episode we've done to date. The segments we've flagged for promo trailers are gold."

"There are also rumors that you're involved in a...*personal* relationship with the property owner's grandson?"

Her muscles tensed as cold seemed to spread throughout her body. "I don't think that's any of your business, Duncan."

"It is if you conspired with your boyfriend to defraud the network on behalf of his grandmother."

She was so stunned by that allegation she couldn't even speak for a few seconds. And when she did, her voice was shaking with rage. "You have got to be kidding me, Duncan. That's utterly ridiculous and you know it."

"Unfortunately, I have no way of knowing what the truth is, but it's obvious that malfeasance has taken place. You're to cease filming immediately. Pack it up and go home while we figure out what to do, both with you and with Tess Weaver."

"The house isn't finished. We can't just leave it like this."

"You can and you will. That contract was fraudulent and we won't spend another dollar on that property. The crew is on their way to the house to pack up any remaining equipment and if you don't comply, you'll be finding your own ride back to Connecticut because they're leaving."

And then he ended the call before she could say another word.

She stared at the phone in her hands for a few seconds, trying to gather her frantic thoughts and sort them into some kind of order. But her life had just spun into chaos and she'd taken everybody else with her.

Maybe she should text Eryn and have her come outside. The two of them together might be able to come up with a way to mitigate the worst of the damage. There had to be a way to protect Tess. And her crew.

Tears threatened to blur her vision, but she closed her eyes and forced them back. She could fall apart later. Right now she had work to do. But when she opened her eyes so she could send a text message to Eryn, movement caught her attention and she looked toward the house.

And saw Finn crossing the lawn toward her.

Something was wrong. Finn had felt it in the air even before Anna left the house to take a telephone call. His mom had refused to accompany them this morning. She claimed Grizz needed some calm time at home, but he was pretty sure she just needed a break. And the crew hadn't shown up yet. He might have thought they were on some other production task, except Anna and Eryn were obviously waiting for them.

Then she'd gotten the call and disappeared. When he'd caught sight of her through a window, she'd looked upset. Calm, but definitely distressed about something. Even though he knew it wasn't his business, he found himself gravitating toward the door.

He'd admitted to himself that he was in love with her. Of course he was going to be concerned when she was upset. And when the call ended and she looked as if she was about to cry, he went outside and started across the lawn toward her.

But when she saw him coming and he watched her chest heave as her breath caught, his steps slowed.

She looked like a woman who had to tell him something he wasn't going to like hearing, and she really didn't want to.

"Bad news?" he asked softly when he reached her. When she nodded, he put his hand on her shoulder, hoping to comfort her. But her eyes welled up with tears and she dropped her head. "Do you want to talk about it?"

"No," she said. She sniffed and breathed in deeply through her nose before exhaling slowly. "But I have to."

"It's not your family, is it?"

She shook her head. "No, it's…"

She let the sentence die away, and then waved her phone toward the house. And when she stood up straight, making his hand fall away from her shoulder, "Anna, whatever it is you're trying to figure out how to say? Just say it."

She pressed her lips together for a few seconds and then gave a single shake of her head. "I got a call from the network. It's over, Finn."

Every muscle in his body tensed. "What's over?"

"Cody hooked up with a local and they had a few drinks and she told him there is no Bayview Inn—that it was all a scheme that Tess had cooked up and she was making everybody in town lie. He told Mike and when Mike couldn't reach Eryn or me—because Eryn was on the phone with her wife and I was with you—he called the producer asking how we should proceed instead of waiting to talk to me first."

"And how are you supposed to proceed?"

Dread built up inside of him when he saw the defeat in her eyes. "They want us to shut it down and go home, and let them figure it out from there."

Let the *lawyers* figure it out from there, he thought. They were going to go after Gram and there was nothing they could do because she'd sent that application with the fake supporting documents. And she'd signed the contract.

"You're just going to leave it unfinished like this?" he asked.

"He was also told it was going around town that you and I are an item, and they're concerned I was complicit. He accused me of conspiring with you to defraud the network on Tess's behalf."

"He *what*?" Anger clouded Finn's mind. "That's ridiculous."

"It doesn't look ridiculous from behind their desks in New York." She blew out a breath. "I don't *want* to go, but I have to, and you had to know this was a possibility since you obviously knew your grandmother wasn't running an inn. I have to talk to them to see what can be salvaged."

"When you say you have to see what can be salvaged, you mean your career?" He heard the words coming out of his mouth and he knew he sounded angry, but he didn't *feel* it. He felt cold. Numb.

"I might lose my career, yes, and I'd rather not. But I also want to see what I can do to protect Tess."

When she sighed and looked down at her phone again, one thought poked through the numbness. "You don't seem angry."

Her head snapped up. "What?"

"You seem... I don't know. Resigned? You're not angry with Gram. You didn't even ask me if it was true. *You* knew this was a possibility."

That sparked a little anger in her eyes. "Come on, Finn. You can fake the oral history of a building all you want, but businesses leave footprints.

And not just a few pieces of paper that smell like Earl Grey, but filings with the Secretary of State's office. Inspections. Certificates of Occupancy. Literally *any* mention on the internet that predates her application."

"You knew the whole time?"

"Of course I knew." She blew out a breath and shook her head. "No, at first I didn't know Tess was making it all up, but I knew it didn't look legit on the surface and I chose not to go digging too deeply."

Anger was building in Finn's gut, but he did his best to keep his tone neutral, even if it was a bit flat. She'd known he was lying to her the entire time, and he felt like a fool. "You knew and you chose to ignore the truth of it."

"When I saw the name of the town, I felt like it was…a sign, I guess. It was time to start getting answers to some of the questions I had instead of just dwelling on them. Coming to Blackberry Bay to rehab the Bayview Inn meant I could try to learn about my mother without just showing up and asking questions about her. I didn't have to tell anybody."

He heard her words, but while his rational mind was trying to make sense of them, the angry part of him latched on to the bottom line. "You knew. You put my grandmother in this position because you needed a flimsy excuse to find your mother?

You could have stopped this before it went this far? Before she got in this deep?"

Surprise flared in her eyes, followed by dismay and maybe even a little anger. "I did not put your grandmother in *any* position. Tess knew full well what she was doing and there's nobody to blame for her situation but herself."

"But you could have stopped it. You could have passed over her application and chosen another property and we wouldn't have had to play this ridiculous game for the last two months. A game my grandmother is going to pay dearly for losing, I might add."

"You can try to paint me as the bad guy here all you want, Finn, but it doesn't change the fact your grandmother knew what she was doing. Joel and Alice knew what they were doing. *You* knew what you were doing. Your entire family was complicit in this." She pointed at him. "She lied. *You* lied. All I did was not expose those lies."

Even if there was some defense he could offer, he wasn't sure he could get the words out because the pain was pushing up through the anger now.

He'd fallen for this woman—he *loved* her—and here they were. Secrets revealed. Lies exposed. This was the end and his heart was breaking, but he needed to focus on Gram right now.

"She defrauded your network. But so did you. Knowingly. And she's the one who's going to pay for it. Your career might take a hit, but she's going to lose everything." He shook his head, as if he could deny they were spiraling into the worst-case scenario. "It's over. I have to…it's done."

"Finn, don't…" She stopped, her eyes pleading with him to understand. "Let's talk this through. We can figure something out."

"You already told me you have to shut down and go home, so there's not much to figure out." He swallowed past the lump in his throat, forcing himself to get the rest of the words out. "Get your people here so you can get you and your stuff out of my grandmother's house."

She closed her eyes as her head dropped again, and he made himself turn and walk away so he couldn't give in to the surprisingly strong temptation to pull her into his arms and hold her until they both felt better. It was over, and it had to be a clean break or he wasn't sure how he'd let her go.

Getting on his bike and doing ninety miles an hour in any direction out of Blackberry Bay was his next choice, but he couldn't do that, either. No matter how much it hurt, he had to be here for Gram. He would be the one to tell her it had all fallen apart.

Anna moved through the massive house room by room, ostensibly looking for anything left behind, but she was really saying goodbye.

She'd fallen in love with this beautiful fake inn. She gave a little piece of her heart to every historical building she worked on, but this one was different. She'd developed a relationship with the old Victorian that existed outside of the family and outside of the show. Not seeing it finished was going to haunt her for a long time.

And the people, she thought. Tess. Joel and Alice. Fierce little Grizz. She cared for all of them so much she wasn't sure she would be able to say goodbye even if they gave her the chance.

Finn. She hadn't expected to fall in love in Blackberry Bay.

She clenched her hands into fists, her fingernails digging into her palms, to distract herself from the tears that wanted to fall. When she finally allowed herself to cry over losing what she'd found with Finn, she was going to cry hard and she was going to cry for a long time. This was neither the time nor the place.

When she heard footsteps approaching behind her, she tensed, but the disappointment crushed the hope almost immediately. They were far too light to be Finn's footsteps.

She turned and was surprised to see Tess coming toward her. A very spry Tess, actually, who was standing tall and wearing shorts and a white T-shirt with a glittery pink flamingo on it. The large polyester housedress she'd been wearing dangled from her hand.

"These things are hot as Hades," Tess said, holding it up. "I am never wearing one again, no matter how old I get to be."

Anna wasn't sure what to say. She'd been worried about Tess since Finn had gone in to break the news to her, and was hoping to see her before she left. Apparently she was finally seeing the *real* Tess Weaver.

"I'm sorry," they both said at the same time, and Tess laughed.

"Don't you be sorry," Tess said. "I dragged everybody into this, and to be honest, I never thought it would go this far. When I got accepted, I decided to take it a little further and then I just... I really hate when Alice is right."

"I won't tell her you said so."

Tess smiled for a moment, and then her eyes grew serious. "I want you to know one thing, honey, because it's been weighing on me. I had no idea you were Christy Nash's daughter when I sent in my application. It's one thing to manipulate what seemed at the time like a faceless corporation with deep pockets, but I would never have used that family connection to try to lure you here. I didn't know until I saw you in person, here at the house."

"That hadn't even occurred to me," Anna assured her, touching Tess's hand.

She turned her hand over to clasp Anna's. "Not yet, but you might have wondered eventually and now you know."

"Honestly, I cheated a little to get here. Production was going to pass over your property, but I insisted without telling them the real reason why."

"Oh, I knew why you were here as soon as you walked in the door. It's funny, but I didn't catch the resemblance when I watched some episodes of the show trying to get a feel for what you'd like." Tess frowned. "That sounds awful. I *am* sorry I dragged you into this."

"I just told you I went out of my way to get *myself* into this."

Squeezing Anna's hand, she shook her head. "Eventually you would have ended up here anyway, looking for Christy, but I got involved and now you're in trouble at work *and* you and my grandson are at odds."

The mention of Finn made Anna's heart ache so badly she might have rubbed the spot on her chest if Tess wasn't holding her hand. *At odds* was such a mild way of putting the current, disastrous state of their relationship. "And your house isn't done."

"Don't you worry about me. It's close enough to done so Joel and Finn can finish it up. Brady will help, and probably some of their friends."

It felt as if the giant elephant in the room squeezed in between them, creating a wall of silence. Maybe the guys in Tess's life could handle finishing the work, but neither Anna nor Tess knew yet what the network suits were going to do. According to the contract Tess had signed, they could go after her for all the money they'd sunk into production so far, and when you added up the costs for Anna, Eryn and the crew, then threw in the supplies, the campground fees and all the other expenses they incurred, it would be enough to financially devastate her. She'd probably lose the house she'd done all this in an effort to save.

"I can practically hear the wheels turning in your head," Tess said, and then she gave a harsh chuckle. "I try not to worry about a bridge until it's time to cross it."

"Tess, it's a really big bridge."

"Never came to a bridge I couldn't get across one way or another. The thing you need to focus on is going back and doing whatever you have to do to save your show and don't even worry about me."

Of course that was what she *should* do, but it wasn't going to happen. "I don't think I can do that, Tess."

"I got myself into this. I got myself and my family and even you into this and I'm telling you I'll be okay, no matter what. Hell, the worst-case scenario is that I move in with Joel and Alice, and that's not that bad."

Anna was pretty sure Tess's daughter-in-law would disagree, and Alice and Tess living under the same roof would have Joel pitching a tent in the backyard just to get some peace, but she kept that opinion to herself. "I'm going to do whatever I can, Tess."

"Anna?" Eryn called from the other room.

"I guess I should let you go," Tess said. "I'm supposed to be waiting in the garden for you to leave, but I wanted to say goodbye to you."

"Listen, the storage pods are paid through next month, and I'll keep tabs on that, no matter what happens with my bosses. I wish I could do more, but—"

"Anna, I'll be okay. But I want you to promise me one thing."

"Anything," she said, meaning it with all of her heart.

"No matter what happens, I want you to try to keep what you and Finn feel for each other separate from this mess. I know it might take a little time, but you need to forgive each other."

"We kept some pretty big, important secrets from each other, Tess. I don't know if—"

"Nope!" Tess shook her head. "Too late. You promised me anything, so now you have to do it."

Before Anna could respond, Tess wrapped her

in a strong hug. She hugged her back, holding her for a long moment.

Then, at a speed that illustrated how good an actress Tess actually was, she gave a jaunty wave and left Anna standing there alone.

She listened as Eryn and Tess said their good-byes, and then her assistant stepped hesitantly into the room.

"You okay?"

Anna shook her head. "No, I am *far* from okay."

"I think we're done here. Frankie and Jim just loaded the last of their tools into the trailer, and Mike—who I'm never speaking to again, by the way—and Cody packed up the SUV. All they have to do is hook up and they're ready to go."

"I guess we're out of here, then." She sighed and looked around the room one final time before look-ing back at Eryn. She couldn't muster Eryn's level of anger at Mike right now, even though they'd started out together and he'd given his loyalty to the network. She had another man on her mind right now. "Have you seen Finn?"

"No. I'm sorry, Anna. Joel was waiting for Tess when I said goodbye, but Finn's bike is already gone."

The stab of pain made her breath catch in her throat, but Anna just nodded and started walking toward the front door.

He hadn't said goodbye. She hadn't even heard his bike start, and he was just gone.

Eryn took a detour on the way back to the campground, driving Anna up the long dirt road to Christy's house. Taffy and Bean were delighted to have company, and Eryn threw sticks for them while Anna sat with her mother for a few minutes on the porch.

"I'm sorry this ended so badly for you," Christy said when Anna finished telling her what had happened.

"I wanted to see you before I leave," Anna said, her voice thick with unshed tears. "I have to go and things are going to be messy for a little while, but I want to see you again. I want to…be your daughter, I guess. Call you sometimes and see you when I can."

The realization that seeing Christy meant coming back to Blackberry Bay threatened to take her breath away, and she had to concentrate on calming herself to keep from falling apart. Even if Finn went back to his life in Portsmouth, he spent so much time in this town there would always be the chance of running into him. Right now she couldn't imagine a time when seeing his face and not being able to touch him wouldn't emotionally devastate her.

"You *are* my daughter. Always. And I already can't wait to see you again. Maybe when things calm down we can get together. I'm not very good with road trips, but I can get one of the boys to drive me halfway."

"That's a good plan. And there's plenty of room for Taffy and Bean, too, though my yard isn't quite as big as yours. I can probably scrounge up a stick or two, though."

When Anna stood, Christy did the same and took a step toward her. "Can I give you a hug?"

"I would love a hug right now." She was afraid she'd fall apart in a sobbing heap when her mother's arms wrapped around her, but she was able to stay calm and savor the feel of Christy holding her for the first time.

There were a few tears when they said goodbye, and a few might have fallen into Taffy and Bean's fur when she gave them love on her way to the car, but she managed to hold back the worst of it.

All that remained now was packing up the RVs and heading out of town. When she was back in Connecticut, she'd call Duncan and start the process of seeing if she could piece her career back together.

The pieces of her heart, though, were thoroughly shattered. Those she knew she wasn't going to be able to put back together.

Chapter Sixteen

Three days later, Finn walked into his parents'
house for the family dinner he'd been more or less
commanded to attend. It was less a dinner than a
meeting, which was the only reason he'd shown up.
His appetite was pretty much nonexistent, but the
problem of the Bayview Inn wasn't going to go away
while he locked himself in his apartment and tried
to bury his heartache under a mountain of work.

"We're in the dining room," his mom called.
"You're just in time."

He kissed his mother's cheek and rested his
hand on his dad's shoulder for a second before
bending to kiss Gram's cheek.

"Anna called me," she said.

No preamble. No easing into it. Just *bam*—words that punched him in the chest. "When?"

"Just before you got here." When she paused, Finn's hands balled into fists. "She just wanted to see how things are."

"I guess she'd know that better than we would, since they haven't been in touch yet."

"She hasn't heard what the network plans to do yet. She's going to try to do what she can for me, though."

Finn dragged a chair out and sat next to her at the table. "What she could have done was shut this whole thing down before it even got started, instead of putting you in this situation for her own personal reasons."

"Finn Weaver, don't you even start." Her tone was sharp, and he arched an eyebrow at her. He wasn't the one in the wrong here. "She didn't put me in this situation. I did. Maybe you can be upset she was complicit in my plan, but it was *my* plan. Make no mistake about that."

"We need to stop trying to place blame and focus on solutions," Alice said gently, resting her hand on Finn's shoulder.

Then she set a plate of ham steak with pineapple slices and potato salad in front of him before going to her seat.

Since everything he put in his mouth this week

tasted like sawdust, he got the discussion started. "There's a guy on the coast who's been trying to buy my bike from me for a while now. I can get a good price from him and I know he can get the cash together quickly."

"You're not selling your motorcycle." Tess shook her head, her lips pressing into a tight line for a few seconds.

"Gram, you've called it a death machine since I got it. You should be happy to see it go."

"But you love that stupid death machine."

"Not as much as I love you."

Her bottom lip got a little wobbly, but then she took a ragged breath. "I know you love me. And no grandmother ever had a grandson as good as you, but honey…it's not going to be enough. I'm the only one whose name is on that contract, so they can get whatever they get from me."

"We're still waiting to hear back on how much we can borrow against our house," Joel said in a low voice. "He promised me a number by tomorrow afternoon. And a bunch of us will be working at Gram's this weekend, if you can make it, Finn."

"I'll be here. We need to get it done enough so selling it before they can freeze her assets is at least on the table, if unlikely."

"We don't even know how much it adds up to," Tess pointed out. "Even if we could reimburse them for the materials, we don't know how much the crew gets paid, and all the expenses of them staying here this whole time."

"We're not trying to reimburse them for everything, Gram." He reached over and covered her hand with his. "They're going to come at us with a number. All we need is enough to offer them a settlement amount in lieu of fighting it out in court, because their lawyers are expensive and the longer it drags on, the more it costs. They know all you have is that house, so when they weigh what they have to gain against how much it'll cost to get it, I think they'll accept a settlement."

"I'd rather lose that house than have you all give up so much."

"We're going to try to make it so nobody loses anything," Joel said. "But don't forget what I told you. *You* don't talk to them. Preston's number is right next to the phone and if anybody calls you, you give them his number."

"He's not that kind of lawyer," Tess mumbled, and she was right. He specialized in estate planning.

"It's not his specialty," Finn agreed, "but he *is* a lawyer and he knows a lot of lawyers. If it comes to it, he'll help us find somebody. The important thing is that you don't talk to anybody from *Relic Rehab* or the network or production company or whatever."

"Except Anna," she argued.

"*Especially* Anna." Just saying her name hurt. "I know you liked her a lot. So did I, Gram. But if she has to choose between your house and her career…she genuinely cares about you. I know that. But I work in business. I know that at the end of the day, businesses have to put the numbers first or they don't survive. She wouldn't hurt you on purpose, but if you talk to her, you might say something that puts her in a tough position."

"But—"

"It's better if you don't talk to her," he said, going for a firm voice, but his emotions were so close to the surface he felt as if he was choking on them. "It's better if none of us talk to her."

"I know you're hurt, but you sound so bitter." She rested her hand on top of his. "I hope you'll forgive her before she comes back to town."

Emotions flooded Finn, but the one that hit him the hardest was the pain. "I don't think she'll be coming back, Gram."

"Of course she'll come back. Her mother lives here. Her brothers and her nephews. She's going to want to get to know them and it'll be a lot easier for her to come here than for all of them to pack up and head to…where does she live?"

"Connecticut," he answered roughly before his jaw clenched.

He hadn't even thought about that, but Gram was right. Telling himself he'd get over Anna and move on wasn't working right now, but it would eventually. But the idea of turning a corner in Blackberry Bay and coming face-to-face with her, with no warning and no time to brace himself emotionally, was a possibility he wasn't strong enough to consider right now.

"That's not too bad a drive, so she'll probably visit a lot," Gram said, and she sounded pretty happy about it, which made his heart ache.

He wasn't the only one who'd fallen for Anna.

After dinner, which he managed to choke down, Finn grabbed a couple of beers and went to sit in the backyard. Since he wasn't going to make the drive back to Portsmouth tonight, he was going to drink them both while spending some quality time with Grizz.

Sometimes the love of a good dog was the only thing that could make things okay.

After a few minutes, his dad joined him. He was carrying a beer of his own, and he pulled one of the patio chairs closer to Finn's. "I wasn't sure if those were both for you or if one was for me, but I guessed the former and brought my own."

"I don't know if I'm good company right now."

"In my experience, the times a man most wants to be alone are the times he shouldn't be."

"I fell in love with her, Dad." He hadn't meant to say the words out loud, but there was something about the beautiful night and the happily oblivious dog that made him feel as if he couldn't keep the pain shoved down anymore.

"I'm sorry it went down like this, son. If I'd known… I wish I'd told those people the truth the day they arrived. If I'd blown it up then, we'd still have the legal fallout, but Anna wouldn't have been in town long enough to break your heart."

Finn took a long swig of his beer and then scratched Grizz's crazy hair when he came sniffing around to see if the humans had snacks to go with their drinks. It helped, Finn thought. His insides had felt knotted up so tightly that sometimes it hurt to breathe, but the tension was easing a little.

"I broke her heart, too," he said after another swallow of beer. "I could see it. She hurt as badly as I did, but what was I supposed to do? We can't… there's no coming back from this."

"I think you're wrong about that. If it's meant to be, son, you can come back from anything."

As much as he desperately wanted to believe his dad, Finn didn't see how it was possible. There had been too many secrets between them and they had hurt too many people—especially each other.

"I can't separate the *Relic Rehab* mess from my relationship with Anna," he said. "Not if they come after Gram."

He heard his dad's heavy sigh. "She can't be the

reason you turn your back on a future with Anna, if you really believe she's the one for you."

"She is the one, but how can I not?"

"Look, my mother's a handful. She is straight-up a pain in the butt. But I know she loves you so incredibly much she would happily pitch a tent in this backyard and live in it with only the clothes on her back rather than watch you let the woman you love get away."

"I know she would. And I love her just as incredibly much, which is why I have to focus on putting this in our rearview mirror. *All* of it."

"The problem with putting something in your rearview mirror that you're not ready to leave behind is that you might spend so much time looking in that mirror you crash and burn."

"That's pretty dark, Dad," Finn said, scowling at him in the fading light.

"Yeah, I probably should have waited until *after* I drank the beer to go all metaphorical."

Finn laughed, and the sound startled him because he hadn't laughed in days. And rather than ruin the moment, he leaned back in his chair, drank his beer and called Grizz up onto his lap. He'd probably only stay there a few minutes, but he'd take it.

He already knew it was going to be a long night, full of staring at the ceiling and thinking about his dad's words.

Finn needed to keep his eyes on the road ahead—get his family on the other side of this obstacle in their path—but it was going to be a long time before he stopped staring at that rear-view mirror.

Anna hated New York City. She hated the cold glass building the network called home. And she hated the so-called power suit Eryn had talked her into wearing today. She felt stiff and overly formal, but during the elevator ride up to Duncan's office, she forced herself to stand up straight and put her game face on.

They kept her waiting, of course. She'd expected that, and she refused to give any indication it bothered her in the least. They would expect her to be scared. Maybe even cry a little, and plead for their forgiveness.

But she wasn't going to do that. She was going to be strong, and if she felt herself stumbling, she'd be strong for Tess. The stakes were high and what power she had needed to be wielded today.

When she was finally shown into Duncan's office, she wasn't surprised to see several other men already in the room. A couple of other executives from the network and one she didn't know, but assumed was somebody from Legal.

"Please have a seat," Duncan said, his deep voice sounding especially stern.

She sat in the chair he gestured to and folded her hands in her lap. The room was so quiet she was surprised she couldn't hear her heart beating, and everybody was startled when Duncan abruptly cleared his throat.

"We've looked at the documentation Tess Weaver supplied with her application. We also spoke to the intern who was shadowing Eryn Landsperger during the meeting in which the team dismissed her application and you vetoed that dismissal."

"I felt as though some of our projects were too similar to hold viewers' interest. The Bayview Inn and Blackberry Bay brought the kind of challenging renovation and beautiful location people love to see on their televisions."

"It took very little effort to discover there has never been a Bayview Inn in Blackberry Bay and that the documents she provided were fabricated." He leaned back in his chair and folded his hands over his midsection in a way that he probably thought was intimidating, but really just made him look paunchy. "The only conclusion we can draw from the information we have is that you were either complicit in this scheme or grossly negligent in doing your due diligence. Considering not only your personal relationship with the homeowner's grandson, but the fact we have since discovered your family ties in that town, we're leaning heavily toward the former."

"I never had a conversation with Tess Weaver or Christy Nash before the day I arrived in Blackberry Bay to begin filming." She hadn't exactly answered the allegation, but it was the best she could do without outright lying, which was never a good legal strategy.

"The network has lost faith in you, Anna," Duncan informed her in such a somber tone she was surprised a funeral dirge wasn't actually playing in the background. Anna was too afraid of extremely inappropriate amusement at the idea of her termination having a soundtrack to risk opening her mouth, so she simply nodded. "We're pulling the plug on *Relic Rehab*, effective immediately."

She thought she'd been mentally prepared for this moment. Mere seconds ago, she'd been on the brink of laughter. But the finality of his words—*we're pulling the plug*—hit her like a ton of bricks, and she sucked in a breath. It was over.

Relic Rehab was over. Her career was over. The relationship she and Finn had been building was over. She had nothing now.

"Anna?"

Eryn. And the guys. She'd lost them their jobs. And if the network executives were angry enough to cancel her show, what were they going to do to Tess Weaver? She wanted to put her head in her hands and cry, but she straightened her spine and promised herself a cupcake and a glass of wine later if she got through this without losing it.

"We'll need you to sign some paperwork," Duncan continued, giving her something to focus on.

"You can send it to my lawyer and she'll look it over," she said in a firm tone. "What about my crew?"

"They're being informed separately right now."

"You could have let me tell them myself." Not that it would have been easy, but it would have been the right thing to do.

"Ms. Landsperger's being offered a position as Toni's assistant because hers isn't working out." Toni was a great person and had a very popular baking show, so it would be a great job for Eryn, and wouldn't involve travel. "The rest of your crew will be snapped up just as quickly, we imagine."

The other two men nodded, and Anna bit back a comment about Duncan speaking for them as if they were some kind of collective. "That's good news."

With some of the anxiety for the rest of the *Relic Rehab* team eased, Anna's mind turned to the other person with something—or even the most— to lose in this fiasco. "What about Tess Weaver?"

She wasn't surprised when Duncan sighed and pinched the bridge of his nose for a moment. This had probably been quite the headache for them, but she cared a lot more about Tess than she did about the network. Especially now.

"Mrs. Weaver very deliberately defrauded the *Relic Rehab* production team and she went to some effort to do it, as well. She didn't simply misunderstand the necessary qualifications or overstate the inn's historical significance. She fabricated everything with the express purpose of getting a free renovation for her home."

There wasn't a lot Anna could say in Tess's defense since that was exactly what she'd done. But that didn't mean she wasn't going to try. "She's an elderly woman who needed help and she went too far."

Elderly was definitely a stretch when it came to Tess, who was living proof of the adage that age was just a number, but the collective didn't know that. They didn't know her. But Anna did and she knew that, no matter what shenanigans the woman dragged her family into, she was all heart.

Duncan gave her a skeptical look, which was mirrored by the collective. "The woman who pulled off—or rather almost pulled off—this elaborate scheme was certainly capable of reading the documents she signed, which clearly laid out the criteria for selection and the penalties for…this sort of thing."

"I think compassion—"

"We're not in the business of compassion, Anna. We're in the business of making money."

And they made that money with a network devoted to feel-good home and family programming, but she knew it was futile to appeal to his sense of humanity. If she was going to have an impact, she had to hit him in the wallet.

"Do you have a number?"

Duncan blinked. "A number?"

"Have you calculated the damages caused by Mrs. Weaver?" When he started to open his mouth, she held up her hand to stop him. "And I'm not talking about some number you pulled out of thin air. I'm talking about actual damages. Production costs and supplies."

"It's not really any of your concern at this point."

"The number, Duncan." She lifted her chin. "Right now you think you have all the power, but I'm the face of *Relic Rehab*. You're the invisible man behind the curtain. The audience is mine, so you can see that it's in everybody's best interest that we part amicably. In order for that to happen, I need to see that number."

He sifted through the papers on his desk and then handed her a sheet of calculations some intern must have written up for him. After scanning the list to make sure nothing that would be a reach had been added, she looked at the bottom line.

It wasn't as bad as she'd feared, so she might be able to get Tess out of this after all. She pretended to go through the list again, item by item, to give herself time to get her thoughts together.

"The total seems reasonable," she said, handing the paper back to him. "Now I want you to think of another figure. What the network's lawyers charge by the hour."

Duncan actually laughed—a mirthless, smug sound that grated on Anna's nerves. "A woman who can't afford to update her kitchen certainly can't afford to fend off our suit, never mind countersue."

"No, she can't." Anna smiled, folding her hands in her lap. "But I can."

The collective let out a sound of masculine disapproval, which didn't faze Anna at all. After a few seconds, Duncan leaned forward and folded his hands on his desk. A power move that also didn't faze Anna. "I think you'll find you don't have any legal standing in this matter, Anna."

"And I think you'll find I don't care, Duncan." His eyes widened, but she made sure she kept her expression neutral. "If you don't simply write off the Bayview Inn expenditures as a loss and leave Mrs. Weaver alone, I'm going to take you to court. I'll fight my firing. I'll fight the papers you want me to sign. I'll demand an audit and then fight over every penny. I'll fight over the brand. Intellectual property. Residuals. I'll wage a very public war, doing the talk show circuit to tell my heartwarming story of finding my birth mother and brother, but how it's tarnished because this network fired me and is trying to take everything a nice old lady owns. You may have facts. But you know how I play with audiences. It's why you brought me here."

Duncan leaned back in his chair, eyes narrowed. "You won't win."

"Maybe I will and maybe I won't. But you and I both know a legal battle with me will cost you more than what a couple months of lost shooting time will."

If there had been a clock on the wall, quite a few seconds would have ticked off before one of the other collective members leaned over and wrote something on the blotter in front of Duncan.

Hope shot a burst of adrenaline through Anna, but she didn't let it show. For all she knew, the note said to tell her to go hell. But she didn't think so. If they were going to stay the predetermined course of firing Anna and suing Tess, the other guy wouldn't have intruded on the process.

"I'm sorry it's come to this," Duncan said, with real regret in his voice. "We loved *Relic Rehab*."

"I'm sorry it's come to this, too. I loved being here." Anna cleared her throat and then made a what-are-you-gonna-do gesture with her hands.

"But it doesn't change where we are now. And it doesn't change my position on the matter."

"You've made your position very clear." Steepling his hands in front of his mouth, Duncan stared down at the handwritten note for so long the silence grew awkward, and then back at her. "I think we'll be able to come to an agreement."

Anna had spent too many years on camera to allow the relief to show, but on the inside she was melting right off the chair and into a boneless, relieved puddle on the floor. "I'm glad to hear it. I'd like to have a final answer on this, in writing, by noon tomorrow."

Her nerves could only take so much. And she was sure every member of the Weaver family was losing sleep over the matter, too. She'd like to be able to put Tess's mind at ease as soon as possible.

And Finn's. She knew he'd be tying himself in knots on his grandmother's behalf. And maybe he was losing sleep missing Anna, too. She sure as hell was. Between Finn and Tess and her job, she wasn't sure she'd slept more than a few restless hours each night since it all fell apart.

"I'll be in touch tomorrow morning," he said before rising to his feet to signal the meeting was over. There was nothing left to say, so Anna stood and forced herself to shake his hand when he extended it. "I really am sorry it came to this, Anna."

"Me, too." Tears welled up in her eyes, but she

was able to blink them back. "I've really loved making *Relic Rehab*."

"As did we. Good luck with your future endeavors."

She made it as far as the elevator before a tear slid down her cheek, and she rested her head against the back wall.

Once she had the document from Duncan that kept Tess and her home safe, she would call the Weaver house and give them the good news. She couldn't imagine the stress they were under and she wanted to ease that, but she knew lawyers and she wouldn't tell them until she had it in writing.

Tonight, she'd have that glass of wine and start thinking about what she was going to do with the rest of her life. She knew what she *wanted* to do. She wanted to spend the rest of her life with Finn. Start a family. Get a dog. But he'd made his feelings very clear.

He hadn't even said goodbye.

No matter what happens, I want you to try to keep what you and Finn feel for each other separate from this mess. I know it might take a little time, but you need to forgive each other.

The promise she hadn't quite made to Tess, despite her insistence she had, echoed through her mind.

Anna had nothing to forgive. One of the things she loved about him was the way he loved his family with his whole heart. She couldn't hold the lengths he'd gone to for Tess against him. Not after seeing them together for two months.

But even if Duncan came through and Anna could tell them it was over and behind them, she wasn't sure if Finn would ever be able to forgive her for the part she'd played.

She had to accept that, no matter what her future held, it might not be shared with the man she loved.

Chapter Seventeen

Brady opened his front door looking as though he'd sleepwalked down the stairs from his bedroom. "It's six thirty in the morning, Finn."

"I thought electricians were early risers. You guys can't make fun of white-collar banker's hours if you keep them, too."

"That might be true for an electrician who wasn't up half the night with a cranky kid because his wife is a *very* early riser who has to help her mom open a bakery before opening her garage for business."

"Can I come in?"

"You didn't even bring coffee with you, man. I'm seriously rethinking this whole best friend thing right now." But he turned and walked toward the kitchen without slamming the door in Finn's face, so he took that as an invitation.

Brady brewed himself a cup of coffee and sat at the table to sip it while Finn made himself one. Once they were both seated, Brady made an "okay, let's hear it" gesture while continuing to drink.

"I need Anna's home address."

Brady's eyebrows arched as he set down his mug. "If you don't know where she lives, she probably didn't think you needed to know."

"I know where she lives. The town, anyway. I just don't have her street address. I guess sending Christmas cards hadn't come up yet."

"Don't be snarky to the man you dragged out of bed at an unreasonably early hour. Are you trying to send her flowers?"

Finn snorted. "I'd have to send her an entire greenhouse just to put a dent in the apology I need to give her. I'd rather say what I need to say in person, so at least she can see that I mean it."

"What are you going to say?"

He shrugged, staring down into his mug. "I don't know exactly what yet. I know I want to tell her I love her. I know I want to tell her I'm sorry I was a total jerk when they canceled the renovation. And I know that's going to be a mess for a while and probably a hard thing to have between us right now, but we can get past it. I just need to know where to find her."

"This is a fun predicament you've put me in. You've been my best friend since we started school. Anna's my sister. And maybe I've only known her a couple of months, but…she's my sister. I don't know what I'm supposed to do here."

"I just need her address. I figured if you don't have it, maybe your mom does."

"And you think I'm going to give it to you? You broke Anna's heart."

"I told you I want to fix that. I *need* to make things right with her, Brady. Even if she can't forgive me, I don't want the anger and fear I vented at her to be the way things end between us."

"As her brother, I feel like it's my job to say you should call her first and not just show up on her doorstep."

"But as my friend?" When Brady only shrugged, Finn sighed. "If she sends me to voice mail or answers and tells me not to come, I might give up. I love her, but I might not be strong enough to try again if she says she doesn't want to talk to me."

They drank their coffees in silence for a few minutes. It stretched on so long that Finn was afraid his friend wasn't actually going to give him Anna's address. And he'd have to respect his friend's decision, if that was the case. It would make it harder for him to find Anna, but he'd drive up and down every road in her town if he had to, looking for her name on a mailbox.

"If it was anybody else, I wouldn't do it," Brady finally said. "But I've known you your whole life and I trust you."

"Thank you."

"But," Brady continued, "if she sees you and still doesn't want to talk to you and tells you to go away, you better go away. I mean it, Finn. If you don't respect what she tells you, no amount of friendship between us will keep me from finding you."

His friend was very serious, and it just made Finn respect him more. "If she tells me to leave, I'll leave. I just feel like I'm only going to get one chance and over the phone just isn't going to cut it."

An angry baby shout from upstairs made Brady sigh. "We're going to be in trouble when he learns his first cuss words. I'll be back in a minute."

It took Brady more than a minute, but Finn used the time to try to calm his nerves. He had a long ride in front of him, and this third cup of coffee probably hadn't been a good idea. But he hadn't wanted to wait. He wanted to see Anna *now*.

When Brady walked back into the kitchen with his son in his arms and his phone in his hand, Finn pushed his coffee mug out of the way just in time for Parker to throw himself at him.

"Hey, buddy," he said, and he chuckled when Parker launched into a recitation of everything he had to tell his uncle Finn since the last time he'd seen him. Finn understood about three words of it, but he nodded and made appropriate sounds of appreciation while Brady made him breakfast.

Once the kid was locked in his high chair with a sippy cup and a bowl of something that looked really unappetizing, Brady slid his phone across the table so Finn could see the information on the screen. He typed the address into his own phone with a hand that was shaking slightly.

"You're a mess," Brady said as he took his phone back.

"She's the one," Finn said quietly.

"I really hope you can work it out. I like you two together."

"I like us together, too. I want that for the rest of my life."

The deep rumble of a slow-moving Harley-Davidson engine cut through the action movie Anna had put on for background noise, and she felt the same pang of sadness, regret and heartache that got her every time Finn crossed her mind.

There were other motorcycles in the neighborhood, of course. But she'd spoken to Tess not long ago, and ended up on speakerphone. As tears of relief were shed, she heard Joel and Alice's voices, but she didn't hear Finn.

"I'll have to tell Finn right away," Tess had said toward the end of the call. "I don't want him selling that death machine of his before I get a chance to talk to him."

"He's not around?" Anna had asked, trying to keep her voice as neutral as possible. She was shooting for polite interest, but even to her own ears, it sounded more like sad puppy dog.

"He left hours ago," Tess told her. "Fired that motorcycle up before anybody else was even out of bed. Don't know where he went."

Maybe knowing that was why her heart beat faster in her chest as the rumble grew louder. And then it stopped. In her driveway.

She started shaking as emotions clamored for the top spot. Hope was winning, but she tried to keep it in check as she walked to the window.

Finn was here. That was really him, leaning the heavy bike onto its kickstand. He took his helmet off and tousled his hair with one hand, which just made it stand up more. Her hand itched to smooth it for him, and she curled her hands into fists.

He pulled his phone out of his pocket and looked at the screen for a few seconds before putting it back. And then she watched him take a long, deep breath before he started walking toward the door.

Anna reached the door before he got a chance to

knock, but he'd reached the top step so they were eye to eye when she opened it.

"Anna."

That was all he said, but she could see in his eyes that he was feeling the same things she was. Regret. Hope. Anticipation. Fear. And that spark of joy she felt just from seeing him again.

He opened his arms and she practically threw herself against his body. He was trembling, too, and she squeezed him with the side of her face pressed against his chest. His heart was racing and a tear slid down over her cheek as he pressed a long kiss to the top of her head.

She had no idea how long they stood in her doorway, holding each other, but she didn't care if anybody was watching.

The words *I love you* were on the tip of her tongue, but some sensible voice in her head held them in check. No matter how good it felt to have his arms around her again, she didn't know yet why he was here. Just because seeing her had made him emotional, it didn't mean he wouldn't walk away from her again.

Maybe he wanted to plead his grandmother's case in person. Since he'd left before she got the news from Duncan and he'd told her once before that he rarely took notice of his phone when he was on the bike, he probably didn't know that issue had been resolved.

"Come in," she said finally, stepping out of his embrace.

"I'm sorry to show up like this," he said, his voice slightly rough. "I needed to see you and I wasn't sure if I called if... I just needed to see you."

"Do you want to sit down?"

He shook his head. "Not really. I want to—"

"I had a meeting yesterday with the network collective," she broke in. She needed to put the Bayview Inn to rest because if they were going to talk, she didn't want that between them anymore.

"Collective?"

"Oh, it's just what I call them, I guess. And they said—"

"Wait." He practically barked the word, so she stopped talking and waited. And waited.

And waited. "What am I waiting for, Finn?"

"Don't tell me about your meeting yet. I didn't listen to the voice mail that Gram left on my phone while I was on my way here. I have something to say to you and I want to say it before you tell me what happened. I want that—the mess with Gram—to be separate from this."

"Separate from what?"

"Us."

That single word made her breath catch in her chest. *Us.*

"It's important to me that you know that what I

want to say to you has nothing to do with whatever happens with the house. This is about you and me, and nothing else."

"Okay," she said so quietly she wasn't sure she made an actual sound.

"I am head-over-heels crazy in love with you, Anna," Finn said. She put her hands to her mouth, pressing her fingers against her trembling bottom lip as tears rolled down her cheeks. "I needed to come here so I could tell you that."

"I am so madly in love with you, too," she whispered. "It doesn't even make sense, but it's the truth."

The corner of his mouth quirked upward in a crooked grin. "This is my first and only time, so I'm no expert, but I've gotten the impression over the course of my life that love doesn't really make sense."

"Is this the part where you kiss me?" she asked, taking a step toward him.

"Almost." But he did reach out and take her hand. "I'm sorry. I was a wicked jerk the day you got that call from the network. I reacted badly and I took all the fear I had for Gram out on you. It wasn't your fault and I'm truly sorry I blamed you."

"I'm sorry, too. I *did* take advantage of Tess's application to have an excuse to go to Blackberry Bay. Once I was there and saw the impact it was having on your family, it was too late to get out of it. All I could do was try to make it work."

He tugged her a little closer. "No matter what comes of it, I want you and me to put that behind us. I want us to be together, Anna."

"I do, too. No matter what."

He kissed her then, his mouth claiming hers as though to make up for the time they'd lost. She stood on her toes, her fingers curled in his hair. He kissed her until she was out of breath and she didn't even care. She just wanted more of him. *All* of him.

When he broke off the kiss and stared into her eyes, brushing her hair back from her face, she could feel the love radiating out from him and her heart felt whole for the first time.

"You know what we should do now?" she asked, grinning at him.

"Oh, I can think of something."

"You should listen to that voice mail from Tess."

His grin faded. "That's definitely not what I was thinking."

"Trust me."

When he pulled the phone out of his pocket, she led him over to the couch and they sat down. She curled against him as he hit Play and put it on speakerphone.

"You woke up the whole neighborhood with that death machine this morning," Tess said, and

Anna chuckled. "Anyway, Anna called and she got the network people to pretend the whole Bayview Inn thing never happened, so you can keep your motorcycle. And I hope you didn't answer when I called because you're out on a long ride. To Connecticut. Bring her back with you, okay?"

As his grandmother spoke, the tension seeped out of Finn's muscles. Anna could practically feel his muscles relaxing, and the long breath he exhaled seemed to clear away the last of it.

"How did you do that?" he asked, taking her hand in his.

"They're smart men. They knew that me fighting them in public would cost them more in the long run than what went into the Bayview Inn."

"What about your show?"

"That's over."

His thumb stroked the back of her hand. "I'm sorry, Anna."

"Me, too. But I don't think I can really regret what happened. Look what I got in return."

He chuckled and kissed the top of her head. "What are you going to do now?"

"I'm not sure. I have the book coming out. Maybe I'll write another. I could do freelance design work. I have enough savings so I don't need to jump into anything."

"I have a crazy thought."

"Just one?"

He chuckled. "For now. That master suite at Gram's with its own bathroom and sitting room? I was thinking about moving in there."

"Really?" She picked her head up so she could see his face. "What about your business? And your place in Portsmouth?"

"I've been doing my business remotely with some commuting for a couple of months and it works for Tom and me. And I'll let the apartment go. I'll bunk at Tom's house if I have to spend the night in Portsmouth."

"That would make it so Tess can stay in her house without worrying about the upkeep or the expense, because, let's face it, she's not really cut out to be an innkeeper." They both laughed. "But it will only work if you really think you'll be happy there."

"I don't think I ever really wanted to leave Blackberry Bay, so I think I'll be happier. But the only way I can be *sure* is if you join me."

"Finn Weaver, are you asking me to be the first honorary guest of the imaginary Bayview Inn?"

He stood up and tugged her to her feet. "I'm asking you to be my wife."

Standing in front of Finn with her hands in his, Anna saw their future flash through her mind. Together in the house they both loved, their lives made fuller in the best possible way by sharing it with Tess. They'd raise their children there and get a dog. They'd be surrounded by his family. And her family. She would spend every day of the rest of her life with this man.

"Yes," she whispered. "Yes, I want to be your wife."

He kissed her until everything faded away except this man—the man she was going to spend the rest of her life with.

"I love you," she whispered against his mouth.

"I love you, too. And I can't wait for us to go home together."

Epilogue

"I heard your mother say it's almost time to cut the cake," Anna whispered in Finn's ear. He was her husband of one hour and forty-five minutes, and she figured they had at least a couple hours to go before they could be alone.

"Which one?" he whispered back.

She laughed, the sound traveling across the sprawling yard and making their guests turn to look. "I can't believe we have three wedding cakes."

"I can't believe they're all carrot cakes," he replied, hooking his arm around her waist so he could pull her close.

"You need to prepare yourself for the inevitable judging after the cake," she warned.

"It's our wedding, not the county fair."

She laughed. "It's cute you think that matters."

The wedding planning hadn't been difficult. They would be married at home—having moved in two months ago when the renovations were completed. They were in the upstairs suite, with Tess in her downstairs room, and none of them had regrets. Anna and Tess got along amazingly well, and Tess did her best to let them have their space. And Finn and Anna would be working on filling the other room with a growing family very soon.

Anna was wearing a traditional white gown that hugged her body and Finn wore a tux, though they'd invited their guests to dress casually for the outdoor wedding. Most of them had ignored that. The flowers were simple and from the florist in town. All in all, *most* of the planning had gone smoothly.

Except for the wedding cake.

As the premier baker in Blackberry Bay and the mother-in-law of the best man, Jenelle Bishop intended to make them a traditional but elegantly decorated carrot cake. Tess claimed her carrot cake was better and she should get to make the wedding cake since she was hosting the wedding, along with the bride and groom. When Alice pointed out that Tess used *her* recipe and didn't make it as well, her mother-in-law challenged her to prove it.

So Finn and Anna had three wedding cakes and all she could do was hope they managed to escape the reception before one of them asked which was best.

Finn snorted. "If they had asked us, I would have voted for chocolate."

"I think there's a rule about New England weddings in the fall having carrot cake." She stood on her toes to whisper in his ear. "But you were smart enough to marry a woman who stopped at Bishop's and bought two double chocolate his and hers wedding cupcakes, which are hidden very well in our bedroom right now."

He growled and pulled her hard against his body. "I love the way you think, Mrs. Weaver."

The sound of silverware clinking against glasses caught their attention and they gave their guests an obligatory kiss. The not-so-obligatory kisses would be saved for later.

"I didn't know it was possible to be this happy," he whispered against her mouth, and tears blurred her vision. There had been several bouts of happy tears over the last couple of days as their friends and family arrived to celebrate their wedding with them.

"Let's stay happy by putting off the cake cutting as long as we can," she suggested. "Let's mingle and try to be hard to pin down. Avoid your mother, your grandmother and Jenelle."

Laughing, he threaded his fingers through hers and led her into the crowd of guests. "You think like a Blackberry Bay native."

They made their way through the guests, stopping and chatting for a few minutes before moving on. Everybody was in a celebratory mood, and there were lots of smiles and a few happy tears.

Her family was there. All of them. While they weren't all sitting together at the long folding tables under the rented canopy, her father had walked her down the aisle. Christy and Naomi were both mothers of the bride, and her sisters had been her bridesmaids. Her parents. Her sisters and her brothers. Her nephews. Her heart was full of love for all of them, and having them all here to witness her marrying the man she loved made her feel whole in a way she hadn't for a long time.

And Eryn had traveled from Connecticut with her wife and their son to be her matron of honor. Their friendship hadn't ended with the end of the show, and they were in almost constant contact. And because Eryn and Tess got along so well, she and Kelly were going to stay at the house for the week Anna and Finn were away and have a true family vacation in Blackberry Bay.

Anna and Finn sat for a while at the table where their best friends had congregated. When setting up for the wedding, they'd cleared a space for the kids to play, complete with a few outdoor games and a playpen in the shade. Brady and Reyna were there with Parker, who had mastered walking and refused to stay in one place. Their friends Cam and Meredith had Sophie and Carolina with them, though Carolina was asleep on a blanket under the table. She was one of those toddlers who went full speed, dropped for a nap, then got up going full speed again. CJ and Benny were playing trucks, and Sydney's kids were playing with the little ones, too, even though they were a little older. Weddings were boring for the preteen set.

"My mother's coming this way," Reyna said after they'd been sitting for a few minutes.

"If you dive under the table, don't fall on Carolina," Meredith said, and everybody except Anna and Finn laughed.

"When are we having cake?" Brady yelled to Jenelle, and because she was looking their way, Anna couldn't even throw anything at him.

"You're going to pay for that," Finn warned his best friend, but she could hear the laughter in his voice.

He stood and took Anna's hand as she pushed off the folding chair. She smiled at him and shook her head. "I guess it's time."

"I'm not going to pick a favorite," he said.

"Not today," she said. "But I know you and

you're going to end up telling them each their cake was the best at some point."

"I don't know. Baked goods are serious business in this town." They were skirting around the guests on their way to the cake table, but when they passed by a large tree, Finn tugged her hand and pulled her around to the other side of the trunk. It wasn't exactly private, but it was as close as they were going to get. "One more hour and then we're leaving."

She laughed. "One more hour and we can *start* leaving. It'll probably take at least that long to say goodbye to everybody."

"Let's just get on the bike and go. They'll figure out we're gone at some point.

They were taking his Harley over to Maine, and then riding up the coastline to a cottage on the rocky beach they'd rented for a week, and Anna couldn't wait.

"We're going to be so exhausted we'll probably sleep for the first half of our honeymoon," she said.

"That's fine as long as I'm sleeping with you next to me."

When he bowed his head to kiss her, she felt the familiar rush of joy and love. "You're right. We'll just get on the bike and go."

"Seven days alone."

"And we'll *have* to spend most of that time in

bed since we can only fit a couple days' worth of clothes in the bags on the bike," she pointed out.

"One hour." He grinned. "We sneak off, eat our cupcakes and hit the road."

"I like the way you think, husband." The glow in his eyes when she said the word matched what she felt, and she squeezed his hand. "I love you, Finn."

"I love you too, wife of mine. Forever."

She kissed him, one long and sweet kiss, and then she gave him one of those crooked smiles he loved so much. "Let's go eat some carrot cake."

* * * * *

#2821 HIS SECRET STARLIGHT BABY
Welcome to Starlight • by Michelle Major
Former professional football player Jordan Shaeffer's game plan was simple: retire from football and set up a quiet life in Starlight. Then Cory Hall arrives with their infant and finds herself agreeing to be his fake fiancée until they work out a coparenting plan. Jordan may have rewritten the dating playbook...but will it be enough to bring this team together?

#2822 AN UNEXPECTED FATHER
The Fortunes of Texas: The Hotel Fortune • by Marie Ferrarella
Reformed playboy Brady Fortune has suddenly become guardian to his late best friend's little boys, and he's in *way* over his head! Then Harper Radcliffe comes to the rescue. The new nanny makes everything better, but now Brady is head over heels! Can Harper move beyond her past—and help Brady build a real family?

#2823 HIS FOREVER TEXAS ROSE
Men of the West • by Stella Bagwell
Trey Lasseter's instant attraction to the animal clinic's new receptionist spells trouble. But Nicole Nelson isn't giving up on her fresh start in this Arizona small town—or the hunky veterinary assistant. They could share so much more than a mutual affection for animals—and one dog in particular—if only Trey was ready to commit to the woman he's already fallen for!

#2824 MAKING ROOM FOR THE RANCHER
Twin Kings Ranch • by Christy Jeffries
To Dahlia King, Connor Remington is just another wannabe cowboy who'll go back to the city by midwinter. But underneath that city-slicker shine is a dedicated horseman who's already won the heart of Dahlia's animal-loving little daughter. But when her ex returns, Connor must decide to step up with this family...or step out.

#2825 SHE DREAMED OF A COWBOY
The Brands of Montana • by Joanna Sims
Cancer survivor Skyler Sinclair might live in New York City, but she's always dreamed of life on a Montana ranch. And at least part of that fantasy was inspired by her teenage crush on reality TV cowboy Hunter Brand. The more he gets to know the spirited Skyler, the more he realizes that he needs her more than she could ever need him...

#2826 THEIR NIGHT TO REMEMBER
Rancho Esperanza • by Judy Duarte
Thanks to one unforgettable night with a stranger, Alana Perez's dreams of motherhood are coming true! But when Clay Hastings literally stumbles onto her ranch with amnesia, he remembers nothing of the alluring cowgirl. Under her care, though, Clay does begin to remember who he is...and the real reason he went searching for Alana...

HSECNM0221

"We need to get our story straight," she reminded him.

His smile faded. "It's best not to offer too many details.
We met in Atlanta, and now we have Ben."

She turned to face him, adjusting the lap belt as she
shifted. "Your family's not going to question you showing
up with a six-month-old baby? Like maybe you would
have mentioned it to them prior to now?"

One bulky shoulder lifted and lowered. "I told you we
aren't close."

"Your mom not knowing she has a grandchild is a bit
more than 'not close,'" Cory felt compelled to point out.
"Will she be upset we aren't married?"

"I'm not sure."